She Was Trembling And She Didn't Know Why.

Diane met Thomas's intense brown eyes and a shudder of realisation raced through her. She *wanted* him to kiss her again. She *wanted* him to crush her in his massive arms and remind her how it felt to be a woman.

Was that what she feared? That he would do all these things and more if she flew away with him to her brother-in-law's palace in Elbia?

'Say yes,' he said so low, the words were a barely audible rumble across her humble Connecticut kitchen.

Diane looked up at the man who seemed to fill a good half of the room. His eyes were hard with determination.

She drew herself up in her chair. *Now or never*…a persistent voice whispered through her mind. *Take a chance. Grab the ring. Risk your heart. For once in your life, do what feels good!*

'All right,' she forced out at last. 'I'll go.'

Dear Reader,

Welcome to Silhouette Desire!

Excitement is guaranteed with the latest instalment in the WEDDING FEVER promotion, which highlights one special wedding book each month. Anne Marie Winston's *Tall, Dark & Western* shows how a marriage of convenience can stoke the fires of passion.

Baby: MacAllister-Made by Joan Elliott Pickart is another fantastic story from Joan's on-going mini-series, THE BABY BET. Will their innocent unborn child bring two best friends together as a couple?

There is no questioning black sheep Sheikh Jalal's ardour for Clio Blake in *Sheikh's Honour* by Alexandra Sellers—the fifth SONS OF THE DESERT story by this London-based author—but is Clio really destined to be a queen?

Another smouldering, rugged marine meets his match in *The Next Santini Bride*, which is the second of the latest batch of Maureen Child's BACHELOR BATTALION stories—created to indulge all our men-in-uniform fantasies.

Finally, from Sheri WhiteFeather comes *Jesse Hawk: Brave Father*, a new twist on a young love affair which had staggering consequences. And in Kathryn Jensen's *The Earl Takes a Bride* a devilishly handsome aristocratic royal bodyguard whisks his heroine off on a luxurious trip—but there doesn't seem to be much relaxing going on!

We hope you enjoy them all!

The Editors

The Earl
Takes a Bride

KATHRYN JENSEN

SILHOUETTE
DESIRE

First published in Great Britain 2001
Silhouette Books, Eton House, 18-24 Paradise Road,
Richmond, Surrey TW9 1SR

ISBN 0 373 76282 8

22-0901

Printed and bound in Spain
by Litografia Rosés S.A., Barcelona

KATHRYN JENSEN

has written many novels for young readers as well as for adults. She speed walks, works out with weights and enjoys ballroom dancing for exercise, stress reduction and pleasure. Her children are now grown. She lives in Maryland, USA, with her husband, Bill, and her writing companion—Sunny, a lovable terrier-mix adopted from a shelter.

Having worked as a hospital switchboard operator, department store sales assistant, bank clerk and school teacher, she now splits her days between writing her own books and teaching fiction writing at two local colleges and through a correspondence course. She enjoys helping new writers get a start and speaks 'at the drop of a hat' at writers' conferences, libraries and schools across the country.

With deep thanks to my wonderful readers,
who loved Jacob, Allison, Diane and Thomas in
I Married a Prince…and wanted more of them.

One

Diane Fields, mother of three, aroused him.

She pushed all the right buttons, as one of his American friends so aptly put it.

She looked at him...and those soft, hazel eyes with a hint of playful sparkle melted his trousers. Worst of all, she made Thomas forget he was employed by Jacob von Austerand, King of Elbia, who had a temper to rival his own and wouldn't be pleased to discover his trusted right-hand man was mentally undressing his wife's sister. Particularly while he was on a royal mission.

Thomas had watched her house for two hours before the lights in the end rooms dimmed and he decided it was probably safe to approach. Nevertheless, he remained behind the wheel of the glistening ebony Benz—concealed behind the glazed windows looking out at Long Island Sound, his strong fingers coiling and uncoiling nervously around the leather-wrapped steering wheel.

He studied the front windows, following telltale wisps of shadows behind them. Was she in the living room or her own bedroom now? He couldn't remember the exact floor plan of the little Cape Cod in this quaint Connecticut town—Nanticoke—a place reminiscent of Chichester on the sea-swept coast of England, where he'd been born.

Maybe he should wait a little longer?

He was stalling for time and he knew it. Thomas cursed softly under his breath and flung open the car door. Straightening all six feet five inches of his muscular body, he rose up out of the leather driver's seat and quietly closed the door.

It wasn't that he didn't want to see Diane, he told himself as he crossed the street. Lord knows he'd been thinking about the long-legged brunette off and on for more than a year and almost constantly for the past two days. Thomas remembered in disturbing detail the lovely contours of her face…and other intriguing parts of her body. Diane Fields was a good-looking woman with a no-nonsense attitude toward life he could appreciate. In her own way she was tougher than her sister, Jacob's bride. Thomas had seen Diane stand up to Jacob on behalf of Allison before His Royal Highness married her. The woman was a force to be reckoned with. But apparently she was in trouble now.

As chief advisor and security officer to one of the most powerful figures in Europe, Thomas Denton Smythe had been dispatched to find out what kind of difficulty the king's sister-in-law was in and how bad it might be. As unofficial royal troubleshooter, he was expected to get to the bottom of things.

Bottom.

Why had he thought of that unfortunately provocative word? He marched forward, smothering a groan. Her bottom, he mused as visions of Diane appeared in his mind, at angles best not dwelt upon.

As Thomas neared the driftwood-gray bungalow, another, fainter light from the interior of the house flicked off. He drew a deep breath and strode bravely across the lawn, already having decided on the side door that led from the driveway directly into kitchen. Logistically it made sense. He didn't want to start off on the wrong foot by waking her children.

Her husband was another reason for using caution. Gary's truck had been conspicuously absent when Thomas pulled up in the sleek black sedan across the street. Even though it was nearly nine o'clock at night, well past the time a construction worker knocked off for the day, there was still no sign of the man.

Before he knew it, Thomas was standing on the four-by-four cement slab outside her kitchen door. There was nothing to do but knock and get it over with.

He waited for her to answer, his arms folded over his chest, wearing the same suit he'd traveled in—impeccable Italian tailoring, but cut much wider than the traditional sleek Continental silhouette to allow for his broad shoulders and muscled chest. He had taken clothes for granted in his younger days. But working for Jacob demanded a certain image.

Hasty, rustling sounds came from behind the door. As if Diane was throwing on a robe…or searching for a weapon before she opened her door at night to a stranger. Now he was certain Gary wasn't around.

Good, he thought. He wouldn't have liked any man who had married Diane, but even with an open mind he hadn't been impressed with Gary Fields. There was something about the fellow he didn't trust.

The white eyelet curtains lifted a bare inch from the left side of the window in the door. An apprehensive fern-green eye appeared for an instant, a sweep of chocolate-brown bangs, then the curtains swung back into place. But the door didn't open.

Thomas cleared his throat. "Diane, it's Thomas Smythe, the king's advisor. It's important that I speak with you."

That did the trick. He heard the latch open. The door jerked wide. Diane stood in a splash of fluorescent light, backed by her kitchen table and a sunflower-yellow decor. She was wrapped in a pink chenille robe. Quickly she pulled it into place when it slipped off one shoulder. Her hair looked damp, as if she'd recently showered and had only bothered to towel dry it. Even from a few feet away, she smelled of strawberries. She smiled in welcome, but looked a little puzzled.

"Thomas, I didn't recognize you. Is something wrong? Are Allison and the babies all right? And Jacob?"

She would have kept rattling off questions at him if he hadn't stepped into her kitchen, nearly filling it. And apparently startling the woman to silence. It was a reaction he often saw from strangers. The intimidation factor of his size was something he actively cultivated in certain situations. After all, he had been responsible for Jacob's safety for many years, and now it was his duty to see to the entire royal family's security.

Unfortunately, in this case, his physique and threatening scowl wouldn't work in his favor.

With effort, he relaxed his shoulders, trying to make himself seem smaller, smiled and put on the charm he usually saved for visiting dignitaries and particularly bedworthy young women. "I'm sorry to arrive unannounced, Diane," he lied in as soft a voice as his rumbling baritone could manage. "I'm in the States on several errands for Jacob, and I hoped you wouldn't mind if I stopped by on my way through."

She smiled up at him, unsurprised, as if people frequently dropped in on her at odd hours. "You've shaved off your beard."

He chuckled. "Do I look very different?"

"Only for a moment," she admitted. "At the window, in the dark. Not many men can make themselves look like James Bond just by shaving."

He never went to films, but he was warmed by her comparison to a movie character she seemed to admire.

"Although," she continued, "you're probably head and shoulders taller than 007."

He grinned, pleased. "Are the children still up?" he asked, knowing they weren't.

"No." She sighed. "They would have loved to see you again. Tommy took an immense liking to you. Maybe because you have the same name. He's grown, you know. You'd be surprised how much, for a seven-year-old."

Although she was smiling and chattering lightly, filling him in on accomplishments and changes in her three offspring—Tommy at seven, Annie, six and

Gare, five—he could read an underlying tension in her nervous movements. Her fingers sought out unnecessary tasks—lining up the salt and pepper shakers on her table, straightening the kitchen towel hanging over the oven door handle. Another sign of anxiety revealed itself in the delicate lines around her pretty eyes and mouth.

He concentrated too long on her mouth, her elegantly shaped lips...and felt himself lean toward her.

She automatically fell back a step as if to make more space for him in the little room. "Do you have time for coffee? Or do you prefer tea?"

"Coffee would be great," he said, although it hadn't been at the top of his list of desires.

She spun around and busied herself with measuring grounds into the coffee maker, fetching milk from the refrigerator, digging two blue ceramic mugs from behind a collection of children's plastic cups in the cupboard. She was offering him her best, though her mugs would have looked common beside the von Austerand's fragile Sheffield bone china.

"May I help with—"

"No, no." She cut him off with a wave of her hand as she transferred the sugar bowl and milk to the table. "Sit, sit. So, tell me how everyone is. Really," she added breathlessly, sweeping damp brown tendrils out of her eyes. She looked suddenly very tired, holding herself together by threads as she swung back to the counter to watch coffee drip into the glass decanter. "Summer in Elbia...it must be lovely."

"You've never been there, have you?" Thomas asked.

"To Elbia? To Europe?" She laughed. "Not likely. Do you realize the cost of foreign travel these da—"

She caught herself, turned to blink at him and smile weakly. "Of course you don't. Everything's on the royal budget, isn't it?"

"Most everything," he admitted quietly.

"Must be nice," she murmured, more to herself, he expected, than for his benefit. She sighed again. "Such an exotic world...far away...the stuff of dreams."

The coffeemaker sputtered out its last drops of dark, fragrant liquid. A pungent aroma filled the kitchen, and Diane pulled herself out of her reverie to fill the mugs and bring them to the table. She sat down heavily, with a little inward sound that wasn't quite a groan.

Thomas watched her as he lifted his steaming mug of black, unsweetened coffee to his lips. It was weak compared to the way he liked it. If they'd been together under different circumstances he'd have shown her how to make a strong European brew to his taste.

He hastily shook away the intimate thought as he watched her add two spoonfuls of sugar and a generous dollop of milk to her own mug. He reminded himself of his mission.

"You look well," he said slowly.

Her eyes were fixed on her beverage. "Absolutely," she said with a chipper lilt that didn't come from the heart.

How to proceed? Thomas felt a little desperate. "I...we, that is, wondered..."

An arrow of suspicion shot through her eyes as they rose to meet his. "So that's what this is." She sounded hurt, and he kicked himself for not handling the situation more tactfully.

"Now, Diane—"

"You've come to spy on me," she accused with a touch of dry humor.

"I'm sorry if I'm intruding," Thomas whispered gruffly. "Jacob and Allison are worried about you and the children. They've received phone calls from Florida. Your parents believe you're having problems of some sort but won't tell them what it's all about."

The touch of anger in Diane's eyes softened. She set her mug down a little too hard, and coffee sloshed over the lip onto the tabletop. "It's nothing they can do anything about. I didn't want to burden anyone unnecessarily."

"I see."

She gave him a look that could only have come from deep sorrow. Whatever had happened must have been pretty awful.

He set down his own mug firmly, hiked himself up even straighter in his chair and spread his huge hands over hers on the table in front of him. "If it's that serious, Mrs. Fields, your family should be told."

"It's nothing that I can't— It's just that—" Something seemed to catch in her throat. A watery glaze covered her eyes, and she looked away from him.

Was she going to cry? He would never have thought it possible. Diane the fighter. Diane the veritable tigress when it came to chasing off the press in the days just after her sister's marriage to Jacob, when no one in either family could go anywhere without a trail of reporters yapping like hyenas at their heels. He'd seen her run off a journalist and his photographer with a broom when the pair had tried to corner her children with questions in their own backyard.

And here she was, an emotional disaster, on the

verge—unless he was mistaken—of breaking down entirely. He didn't have a clue what to do.

"Diane, let them help."

She pulled herself up and stood to face him as he rose from the table. The top of her head only reached the shoulder of his suit jacket. "I'm just tired. Days are pretty long around here. I should go to bed now."

"Tell me what has happened," he said, emphasizing each word.

She looked up at him, a spark of proud fire momentarily brightening her sad eyes. "Please go."

"You are not leaving this room, and I'm not leaving this house until you tell me what's going on."

"Why does it matter?" Her eyes narrowed suspiciously. "It's the possibility of scandal, isn't it? If the press hears the king of Elbia's sister-in-law is bereft of a husband and can't pay her electric bill, they'll have a field day. Won't they?"

Thomas's heart stopped. So that was it. "Gary's…left you and the children?" he asked hesitantly.

"Gone…flown the coop…absconded with a floozy from the office…good riddance." She fluttered a hand carelessly in the air, but the gesture didn't fool him a bit.

"Dear girl, I'm so sorry," he muttered, trying to recover from his shock and think of something…anything appropriate to say.

"Well, I'm not," Diane said in a quiet voice just short of cracking. "It's been a long time coming. I should have insisted years ago…didn't…couldn't find a way to—"

The last ounce of strength drained from her. She

turned with a choking sob and rushed toward the doorway into the living room.

Thomas cut her off with one enormous stride. She ran smack into his chest with her bowed head. His big arms immediately wrapped around her, pinning her there. She struggled for exactly half of one second, then went limp in his bear hug of an embrace.

Neither of them said a thing. But now that Thomas had her in his arms, her trembling body flush against his, he wasn't sure what to do with her.

She didn't push or squirm or indicate she needed space, oxygen or even words of solace from him. She seemed content just to remain where she was.

It was at that moment he became aware of an embarrassing development. Down below his belt. He felt himself move, extend, become...firm.

Thomas squeezed his eyes shut and willed himself to remember he was duty bound to Jacob to protect, defend and honor the members of his family. Desire wasn't supposed to enter the equation. That meant not responding to Diane as if she were a beautiful, soft, desperately overworked woman who might welcome a man. That meant switching off his hormones for one bloody hour, finding out what he needed to know, mending whatever was broken the best he could...and *getting the hell out*.

If he played his cards right and there were no technical delays at the airport, he could be on the royal jet and headed back toward Europe in a matter of hours.

But at the moment a woman was weeping on his chest. Probably ruining his new suit jacket, he thought regretfully. He had paid an exclusive tailor in Florence to make it for him, at the cost of more *lire* than his recent week on the Riviera with a sultry French actress. In retrospect, the suit had seemed the better deal.

Diane made no sound, moved not a muscle. Nevertheless he knew she was crying by the bucketful.

"Mrs. Fields," he said, "I'm good at fixing things. Let me help." Although he'd meant to be gentle, even paternal, his words came out clipped, tense, business-like.

If she hadn't been moving before, now she was suddenly as still as granite, hardly breathing, taut from her tiny bare feet to the top of her shampoo-fresh head. "Help?" she whispered hoarsely. She looked up at him with incredible sadness. "You silly man, this isn't a matter of diplomacy or rescuing Jacob from a mob of overenthusiastic paparazzi."

"I realize that," he began, employing his best diplomatic tone nevertheless. "But perhaps there is a way to work things out between you and your husband."

"No, there isn't." She ducked out of his arms and began pacing the vinyl flooring. "I know it was the right thing to do, signing those papers, but I can't bear to think how my kids are going to suffer."

Thomas frowned, feeling something like panic tug at his gut. "What papers?" Did she mean separation papers? Or was she already divorced? He couldn't walk out without something more exact to report to Jacob. But he also wanted to know, for himself.

"Mr. Fields is where now?" The words came out casually enough, but the muscles in his shoulders and arms bunched, as if prepped for battle with the man who had broken the heart of this amazing woman.

"I don't know and I can't say that I really care."
She smiled grimly at him.

Thomas stared at Diane, hesitant to push further.
Seeing her in such anguish was devastating to him,
although he didn't understand why. Over the years he
had hardened himself to the pain of others. He held
little sympathy for anyone who wasn't part of the
royal family or the inner circle of the court. The von
Austerands had, in every sense but one—blood—become his family.

After all his own parents had deserted him—each
in their own way. He had been barely five years old
when his mother had left his father, the Earl of Sussex, his two brothers and him. At six he'd been
shipped off to a boarding school by his aristocratic
father. Who had bloody well cared about *him* then?

The troubles of strangers were of no consequence
to him. And Diane, though related by marriage to
Jacob, was in all other ways a stranger. Yet, watching
her suffer the rejection of the father of her children,
he felt truly and deeply moved.

"I'm sorry," Thomas began slowly. "He's a fool
to have left you."

She gave him a tiny, appreciative shake of her
head.

"If it's money you're worried about, there are ways
to track down a deadbeat father and force him to do
his share. It's the law in this country."

"I know. I'd just rather do this on my own. They're
my kids. He wouldn't have left if he'd loved them."

Thomas winced. Had his mother not loved him and
his brothers?

Diane pulled the chenille belt tighter around her
waist to close an enticing gap over her chest that

Thomas was having difficulty pretending wasn't there.

"I suppose not," he said, mourning the view now blocked by fuzzy tufts of fabric.

Diane cast him an irritated glance. "You're not going to leave, are you." It was a statement.

"Not until I have something more to tell Jacob."

She whirled toward the living room and disappeared around the corner. He found her digging through a stack of mail scattered across the coffee table among crayons, dried-up bits of modeling clay and miniature dinosaurs in molded multicolored plastic.

She came up with a long white envelope and thrust it at him. "Here. This tells all. Read and relay as much as you like to my concerned family."

Her robe slipped open again.

He ached to kiss her. There. Right *there* between her beautiful breasts.

But she was holding the envelope out to him. Waiting.

Reminding himself of his duty for the hundredth time, Thomas took it from her, extracted its contents and unfolded a five-page document. "It's a divorce settlement—legally signed, dated, notarized." He looked up at her, but whatever emotions he expected to see in her eyes were absent. She'd pulled herself together in the time it had taken him to scan the agreement.

"You've accepted sole custody of the children and released your husband of all financial responsibilities?" He didn't understand. "Why, Diane? Did he coerce you into signing this?"

"No," she said. "I'm the one who filed for divorce and had the papers drawn up."

"And your lawyer…he didn't—"

"He advised me against releasing Gary from his obligations to the children. He said I had grounds to demand support plus a large settlement for emotional injury due to his desertion."

"But you ignored his advice."

She looked him squarely in the eyes. "I don't want anything to do with Gary Fields. The children and I are better off without him."

"No doubt," Thomas agreed. "But still—"

"Don't say another word," she warned, shaking a finger at him as if he were one of her brood. "It's done. Now all I have to do is figure out how to survive on pride…because there sure isn't a lot of money coming into this household."

She started pacing again, this time crisscrossing the oval, braided rug that nearly covered the living room floor. "Listen, Thomas, I wasn't trying to hide anything from Ally and Jacob…or from my parents. Or embarrass anyone. I just didn't want them to worry, you know? I had decided to wait until I was sure of the end result. I didn't know until yesterday's mail that Gary had signed the divorce papers."

"But he did."

"In a heartbeat." She laughed dryly, shaking her head. "He never loved me, not really. I don't think even I know what love is. I was a good wife to him, but now it's finished. And I'm glad, I really am. Neither of us was happy."

"I understand." What still didn't make sense to him was why she hadn't fought for what was rightfully hers. She couldn't possibly support three children on the money she made from her in-home day care business.

She looked up at him from beneath thick, dark lashes. "Sorry, you don't deserve to get dumped on like this. You're just the messenger, right?"

Her fingertips were lightly smoothing the vee of skin between her throat and breasts, unconsciously opening the robe again. He followed their teasing pattern, wishing she'd stop doing that. He was having enough trouble giving a damn about wayward husbands and legal documents. He imagined how her long, delicate fingers would feel sliding down his bare chest, across his belly, descending to—

"We hadn't been intimate for a long time," she continued, more to herself than to him. "Sex just didn't seem very important to Gary."

Personally, he couldn't imagine any man not wanting to be intimate with Diane. "Most married men *are* interested in sex, no matter what else they may say. They just search for a suitable outlet...which may or may not be their wife."

"Outlet. How harmless sounding," she murmured, nibbling thoughtfully at her bottom lip. "Is that all we women are to men?"

He put a hand out to touch her shoulder consolingly but thought better of it and drew his curled fingers away. "Of course not, not where a real man is concerned." But he had a flash of guilt for the women he'd used in the past. Did it matter that they'd used him, as well? For his money, for the gifts, for an entry into glamorous royal functions and a leg up in society? Maybe he wasn't totally innocent, either. "I just meant," he added slowly, "that Gary's character isn't of a caliber to match yours. He didn't deserve you."

She looked at him strangely, as if trying to decide how seriously she should take his compliment. She had stopped keeping track of her robe's antics: one creamy shoulder was bare.

Thomas turned away and stared out the front window at the Benz, parked in a shadowy patch between two streetlights. He drew a deep breath, recentered himself, told himself sternly that his reason for being here was Jacob...not his lovely, tempting sister-in-law.

"May I tell your sister and the king what I've learned tonight?" he asked, his voice restored to its formal, controlled chest rumble.

She didn't answer right away. "Of course. But before you return to Elbia I will have called Allison and spoken with her. I realize they will need to know. I'll also call my parents."

"The children—" he began, but she cut him off.

"Gary never spent much time with them. They obviously miss him, but his absence isn't a big change for them. The money will be tight for a while, but I'll figure out what to do." She sounded confident.

"You're sure?"

She gave him a sunbeam of a smile. "Of course. I'm a survivor, Thomas. If you knew me better, you'd understand that."

He nodded but decided to try one last time. "I have the authority to give you a blank check—"

"Somehow I guessed you would have. Tell Jacob for me, No, but thank you. We'll manage."

There was nothing more he could do. Right? He'd learned the truth and offered assistance, which had been politely refused. If he telephoned the pilot at

JFK, he might still make it back to Elbia by midday tomorrow.

"If you're sure," he said, taking her hand in a gesture calculated to be gentle, friendly, consoling.

"I'm sure," Diane whispered.

Then she ruined everything.

She stepped up to him, rose onto her toes and kissed him lightly on the ridge of his jaw. A feather of a kiss from a woman who had the charity to respond with graciousness toward others despite her own immeasurable grief and disappointment.

"Thank you for coming, Thomas," she whispered. She undoubtedly didn't intend for her breast to brush against his arm as she withdrew. But it did.

He marched to the car, cursing his body for betraying him. One little kiss, one accidental touch, one bare shoulder...and his hormones were bouncing around inside of him like blasted Ping-Pong balls. Now there was no way he could leave for home tonight.

Two

Diane shooed her three darlings outside. Tommy, named after her dad, a retired Amtrak conductor, was leader of the pack. As the oldest child on the street, he was undisputed monarch of the neighborhood. Occasionally his sister, Annie, tricked him into doing what she wanted. But most of the time he saw right through her ploys.

Gary, Jr., known only as Gare from the time he was born, was the baby of her adored litter. He would begin kindergarten in the fall but didn't look old enough. He idolized his big brother, collected dinosaurs and favored chocolate syrup poured over everything. Including mashed potatoes, if she'd let him have his way.

Altogether, they got along well and Diane would have cheerfully welcomed three more of the same. She loved children, so much so that she'd begun a day-care service in her home to enable her to stay home with her own while bringing some money into the house to help with expenses.

She let a nearly forgotten wish pass through her mind. If she could…if she ever had the money, she'd take her children with her on marvelous trips to far corners of the world. They would hike through exotic countries…share delicious foods of other cultures…listen to the music and language and laughter of other lands…and learn about people others called foreigners but she thought of as neighbors.

Dreams. Beautiful girlhood dreams that had been nourished by three years of studying international relations and sociology in college. They would never come true.

Diane put out a hand to touch the door frame and let her eyes close for a moment. The darkness behind her eyelids brought a temporary sense of separation from reality. It was so tempting to stay like this—shut off from overdue bills, from the loneliness, from the knowledge that traveling the world would never come to be.

As fond as she was of Thomas, she'd lied to him the night before. How she was going to make ends meet, she didn't have a clue. Not yet. She had to come up with a plan.

When she opened her eyes, Tommy was helping little Gare onto the swing. Annie was swooping down the slide in their securely fenced yard. The June sun was warm. Unless someone took a spill, they'd be content for at least an hour on their own. And it was Saturday—no day-care kids. Now was as good a time as any to consider her options.

Forty-five minutes later, her checkbook lay open in

front of her on the kitchen table. Checks to cover the most urgent bills had been written, bringing her balance down to almost nothing. In two weeks she'd be paid again, but without Gary's earnings she'd be hard put to continue making ends meet.

Thomas had been right. She'd been too proud to ask Gary for help. But she wouldn't go begging to her ex now. Alternatives. That's what she needed. What were hers?

She could ask her parents for a loan. Or she could reconsider Jacob's blank check. But either one would be a temporary fix at best and leave her feeling indebted to her family. She stood up, stretched and walked across the kitchen to work the stiffness out of her bones. It took making a cup of tea and circling the kitchen table for another ten minutes to come up with the obvious answer: get a better paying job.

That would mean working outside of her home, leaving her children in someone else's care when they weren't in school. Other mothers did it; she could, too. But she felt as if she was breaking a silent promise she'd made to her babies when they were born. She sat down again at the table, convinced she couldn't feel any worse.

A moment later a series of fist-on-wood thuds rattled the glass pane in her kitchen door. She twisted around in her chair with a startled jerk just as Thomas Smythe opened her door without invitation and stepped inside. She was immediately reminded of the deliciously illicit feelings he'd awakened in her the first day they'd met…and every time since.

"I thought you'd have left for Elbia by now," she said, pushing back from the table to stand up.

He shrugged, his shoulders threatening to break out

walls. "I had a few more matters to look into before I left," he said, placing a white paper sack on her table that looked as if it had come from the local bakery. He had only a slight English accent, which she attributed to the amount of time he'd spent in the United States and other countries on behalf of Jacob.

"What kind of matters?" She dug into the bag and brought out an enormous raisin scone. As anxious as he'd seemed to get out of her house the night before, she figured they must have been terribly important to keep him in Connecticut.

"Just details. Like making sure you have enough cash on hand to survive the next few months."

The big guy doesn't give up easy, does he? she thought, amused by his insistence on doing his job, but also a little annoyed at Jacob's interference. "Well, there's nothing you can do if I don't want help, is there?" She took a bite of the scone, then waved it in challenge at him. "Short of dumping truckfuls of cash into my accounts, but you don't have the name of my bank or the account numbers, so…" She nearly choked on a mouthful of crumbs at the mischievous twinkle in Thomas's dark eyes. "You wouldn't. You didn't!"

He just looked at her. He wasn't quite smiling, but she was sure the effort to keep a straight face was costing him.

"Damn you, Thomas. And Jacob, too. It's no doubt his name that loosened tongues." She tossed his raisined peace offering on the table. Men! What right did they have to take over her life? She was perfectly capable of working things out for herself. Surviving the next few months might not be fun, but she'd find a way.

"It's for your own good. In the children's best interest," Thomas explained solemnly.

"Well, you can tell Jacob that I resent his intrusion into my private life!" she snapped. "I don't need anyone's charity."

"You'll lose your house. You'll be on the street," Thomas said calmly.

"The hell I will." She flashed her eyes at him.

"If accepting a gift isn't your preference, consider the money a short-term loan."

She glared at him, but couldn't stay angry. She'd always liked him. What amazed her about Thomas was that he never seemed to think of himself. He was always doing things for Jacob—bringing him documents, keeping him on schedule for his appointments, driving him here and there, protecting him from outsiders. He seemed on duty twenty-four hours a day. And now he protected her sister, nephew and niece as well. He was a little scary sometimes—because of his size and booming voice. But he was, she believed, one of the most honorable and dedicated men she'd ever met.

He continued calmly, his dark eyes fixed on her face. "You have to be reasonable, Diane. If not for your own sake, then for the children...."

She felt silly, turning down gobs of money. Giddiness took over. She did what every first-grader learns to do when confronted with adult logic. She covered her ears, closed her eyes and belted out "The Star Spangled Banner" as Thomas continued his argument.

Halfway through the first verse, Diane was struck by a steamroller of male flesh. She let out a gasp of shock as Thomas forced her up against the kitchen counter, seized her by the shoulders and kissed her fiercely on the mouth.

Diane struggled for precisely two seconds, then went limp against him. Do men really kiss like this? she wondered dizzily, all other concerns driven from her head. His lips were warm and full. He didn't just kiss her, he consumed her. The faint scratchiness of morning stubble added heat to his mouth against hers. His big hands released her shoulders, but only to allow his fingers to rake through her tousled hair. His palms clamped either side of her head and pressed her toward him again, increasing the pressure on her lips.

It felt so good, she thought she would die.

When Thomas finally relinquished his claim to her lips, he pressed her blazing cheek against his shirtfront and breathed heavily for several seconds. She felt the rise and fall of his immense chest beneath her cheek. Heard his heart thudding strongly.

"Is that supposed to satisfy my banker? Or just you?" she asked, her voice unusually husky sounding.

"Both of us—you and me." He ground out the words.

"Uh-uh." She had to catch her breath and refocus her thoughts before she could come up with anything more to say. Through the window over the sink she glimpsed Tommy, Annie and Gare. They'd been joined by two neighbor children and all were now busily digging in the sandbox.

"You started it," Thomas said at last.

"What?" She tried to pull away, but he made no move to release her. "Me? I believe all I did was tell you I didn't want Jacob's money!"

"Last night, woman," he said. "You kissed me."

"But…but that was just an innocent peck on the cheek!" she protested, although she remembered the electricity she'd felt zap between them at the touch of her lips. "It was a gesture of thanks, that was all."

"It was more," he said, sounding irritatingly sure of himself.

"Was not."

Was too, her Tommy would have replied.

But the Englishman said nothing more for another moment. At last he sighed and moved a step back from her, his hands dropping to his sides. "I've never met a more maddening woman in my life."

She decided it would be safer to pretend smugness than to let him see how thoroughly he'd shaken her. "I'll take that as a compliment," she retorted, flashing him a chipper smile.

"It may well be," he murmured, gazing down at her with more intensity than she had ever seen in any man's eyes. "It may well be…Diane." His hand rose from his hip to the level of her chin. She didn't pull away as his thumb caressed the fragile line of her jaw, then touched her lower lip before retreating.

"Did Jacob tell you to offer physical as well as financial consolation?"

For a fraction of a second he looked hurt. Then his expression hardened and he took three stiff steps back from her. "His instructions were to find out what, if anything, was wrong and offer help if that seemed prudent."

"Prudent." She couldn't help chuckling dryly at the old-fashioned sound of the word. "I don't believe what we were doing just now would be considered prudent by Jacob, especially in his present status as reformed-playboy king.''

Thomas cleared his throat, looking more uncomfortable by the moment. ''I'm sure it wouldn't, Mrs. Fields.''

She shrugged. ''Please…we can't very well revert to courtly etiquette, not after *that* kiss.''

Oddly enough she felt stronger, in better possession of her mental facilities in the aftermath of Thomas's amorous onslaught. She was puzzled by this unexpected side effect. Maybe the brief taste of pleasure had syphoned off pent-up energies that had been interfering with her effective analysis of the situation. At the very least she'd been reminded that men and women did, under the right circumstances, interact with passion.

Had Gary even once embraced her with such fervent desire? She couldn't remember. She thought not. No, definitely not. She certainly hadn't felt her body respond as it had when Thomas kissed her. Which was somewhat in excess of cataclysmic.

''I-I'm truly sorry for overstepping my bounds,'' Thomas muttered, avoiding her eyes. ''I was out of line.''

''Yes,'' she agreed. ''You definitely were.''

He adjusted his shoulders, ran his tongue between his lips and seemed to make up his mind to meet her gaze again. ''I've never forced a woman. It wouldn't have gone further than the kiss. I wouldn't even have kissed you if you were still married. Please, forgive me if I've embarrassed you.''

''I forgive you, Thomas.'' Why did everything he say send teasing vibrations through her? ''I suppose you might have been misled by that silly thank-you kiss. I'm not focusing very well these days on other people's feelings. There are so many things still to be resolved, even though Gary's been gone for over six months.''

"That long?" He looked surprised.

"Actually, it seems longer. For the past two years, maybe more, he hasn't been around much at all.''

"I am sorry…truly I am.'' Even now he looked as if he wanted to touch her, but she didn't understand why that should be. Allison had told her something of Thomas's taste for glamorous women.

Nevertheless she stepped around the kitchen table to the other side. Furniture made good defensive fortifications. From this distance she thought she saw a shadow pass over his eyes. It occurred to her she might have hurt his feelings or touched on some hidden injury without realizing it.

"I'm sorry I've been so rude,'' she said apologetically. "I have been very short with you, and I know it. But it's totally against my nature to accept help. I've always been able to fend for myself.''

"Isn't that what your sister was trying to do by keeping her baby to herself?''

Diane remembered as if it were yesterday. She smiled. "At the time, it seemed unlikely the father of Allison's child would ever come back into her life. Who could have known the college boy she'd fallen for was a prince—complete with royal palace and a country at his bidding?''

Thomas smiled, too, looking a centimeter less tense. "At one time I didn't believe Jacob was other than a spoiled rich boy who needed looking after while he was in an English school away from his family.''

"You started working for him that long ago?"

"Yes," Thomas said, pulling out a chair, then motioning for Diane to sit in it.

She sat, then picked up the scone she'd dropped on the table and took another bite. He spotted the pot of coffee on the countertop and poured each of them a cup.

"I'd just come out of the British army after serving overseas. I wanted to stay home for a while in London, see if I could find a decent job...." He winked at her. "Talk a few girls into bed while I was at it. Those were my only goals. Simple ones."

"Simple but laudable for a young man," she commented with a hint of sarcasm.

"Well, they didn't work out. Instead, I acquired a young lad who always seemed to be getting himself into trouble. The first time I saw Jacob, he was at the wrong end of another man's fist, getting beaten to a bloody pulp by a couple of what you Americans call longshoremen. I stepped in to even up the sides, and we managed to walk out of the pub alive.

"He was still in school at the Crenworth Academy and headed, he informed me, for more years of formal education in the United States. His future had been mapped out by his family. He hated not being able to make his own decisions about what to do with his life."

Diane nodded. "I understand." Hadn't so much of her own life been determined by chance?

"To make a very complicated story short," Thomas continued, "Jacob attached himself to me. I don't know why. Maybe because I didn't keep reminding him of who he was, because I really didn't know." He smiled. "But it wasn't long before a crotchety royal chancellor cornered me and filled me in. You could have knocked me flat with a teaspoon. A crown prince. Being prepped to take over the throne of one of the wealthiest little countries in Europe—Elbia. And there I was taking him out to pubs, pulling him out of fights and walking him home, both of us drunk as skunks. I was shocked. I apologized and promised the man I'd never meant Jacob any harm. It was just that I liked him, I really did. And I sort of felt sorry for the lad.''

Diane was amused by Thomas's tale. "Then what happened?" she asked, as he polished off his first scone and reached hungrily for a second from the sack.

"I told the old man I'd make myself scarce. But he says in this German accent you could cut with a knife, 'You vill continue to go everywhere with Jacob. You vill *not* let him out of your sight for as long as you or he lives. The king vill pay you vell to continue protecting his son.'"

Diane laughed at his imitation. This was a piece of palace lore she hadn't heard from Allison. But she couldn't help noticing that Thomas mentioned surprisingly little of his own background before he'd met Jacob, and she made a mental note to ask him about that later. She was curious.

Diane finished her own buttery scone and sat back to lick delicious crumbs from her fingertips while Thomas finished a third pastry. They drank another cup of coffee slowly, in companionable silence. For some reason she had the distinct impression that Thomas's mind wasn't as quiet as his body.

At last he looked across the table at her.

"What now?" she asked. "No more Mr. Nice Guy?"

He frowned. "What?"

"I think it comes from a movie, or maybe a TV show. Don't know which," she murmured, automatically taking in the sounds of play from the backyard. She'd learned to read them so well she could tell the children were safe.

Thomas folded his hands and observed her over the wide knuckles. "Learning to accept help when it's necessary to one's survival is an important life lesson," he said solemnly.

His eyes felt as if they were driving an opening through her body to her heart, making way for his message. She lifted her gaze to the ceiling and sighed. "I see. So what you're telling me is that Jacob intends to help me whether or not I want his help."

"That's right," Thomas said. He reached across the table, lifted a strand of hair from over her eye and tucked it behind her ear. "I'd say you've had a rough six months, at least. You deserve a rest and time to think about what you want to do. It's not just your own life, it's your children's future that is in the balance."

Tears suddenly threatened. She willed them away and swallowed over the tightness in her throat. This was the one argument that had a chance of swaying her. Her children's welfare. She could insist that everyone leave her alone, as long as she risked only her own security. But as soon as Thomas put the situation that way, she couldn't let her pride make decisions that might hurt her babies.

Thomas nodded as if he understood the shift in her mind set. "Good. Your immediate finances can be dealt with in the form of a short-term loan from Jacob,'' he said calmly, his hand rising to stave off an objection she no longer had the strength to make. ''I've already deposited money into your checking account. And—'' he rushed on ''—please don't make so much of this. You have no idea how insignificant a few thousand dollars is to His Majesty. Think of it as a fistful of pennies taken from Fort Knox.''

Diane let out a deep breath. Viewed that way, she was probably being foolish to make such a fuss. ''All right. But it's just a loan.''

''Agreed.'' Thomas looked quietly pleased with the negotiations, though he didn't risk setting her off with a full-blown smile. ''Next of concern—your health and emotional well-being.''

She laughed dryly. ''Believe it or not, money can do nothing to repair a heart that's been stomped flat.''

''I suppose not,'' he admitted, his huge dark eyes lingering compassionately on her face. ''But a change of venue and a break from work might.''

''You mean, a vacation?''

''I think it's time you visited your sister. She misses you, you know. It's not as if a queen can dash halfway around the world whenever she feels homesick or wants to see her family.''

Diane stared at him. ''Fly to Europe? Talk about throwing away mon—''

He reached across the table and laid his hand on top of hers. The heat of his strong fingers closing over hers silenced her. ''Stop thinking about money. I told you, it's nothing. You sound like your sister.''

Diane couldn't help smiling at that, just a little. ''Our parents were very thrifty people. New Englanders generally are. Sorry.''

"Nothing wrong with being sensible," Thomas allowed. "But there are times when cash spent is wisely parted with."

She rolled her eyes. "I have a feeling this is going to cost Jacob more than the proverbial few pennies. Go on."

"I have arranged everything. All you need to do...is agree," Thomas said with almost painful slowness, as if this was a difficult part he'd rehearsed. "Before I came to your house this morning, I contacted your parents in Florida." Barreling onward, he paid no attention to her gasp of outrage. "They would be thrilled to have the children join them for the rest of the summer. I've arranged for Jacob's private jet to take us to Vienna tomorrow night. From there, his helicopter will carry us to Elbia. I felt you might need a day to prepare and pack."

"Generous of you," she commented, not bothering to hide her sarcasm. The nerve of the man! Taking her life into his hands as if he was planning one of Jacob's diplomatic jaunts. "But I could never put my children on a plane and watch them fly off alone."

"That's been taken care of. Allison told me you often employ a young lady named Elly Shapiro, three doors down the street from you. I've spoken with her mother about the possibility of her taking the position of nanny for the summer. In return she'll receive a generous stipend for her college fund."

"And no doubt be thrilled with the chance to spend three months in Florida, away from her brothers and sisters," Diane added. He seemed to have thought of everything. "And what am I supposed to do in Elbia for the whole summer?"

"You'll have the luxury of time to do anything that

appeals to you…other than work. No responsibilities. No budgeting, cooking or laundry. Just time to visit with Allison and your niece and nephew, tour whatever parts of Europe appeal to you, shop for new clothes in the best boutiques, read—"

"Eat!" Diane added, getting into the spirit of the moment, although she still had nagging reservations that she was doing the right thing. Maybe she would only be avoiding the inevitable by allowing Thomas to sweep her off to Europe. "I understand there are a few decent restaurants in Europe…perhaps even in Elbia."

Thomas's eyes twinkled with appreciation for her humor. "So I've been told. Prepare to put on a few pounds…or burn them off as Allison does by including a vigorous, hour's walk in your daily routine."

Admittedly, it did sound wonderful. Too wonderful?

Life just isn't this easy, Diane reasoned sadly. Solutions to problems don't simply fall from the sky in the form of wealth and palaces. Yet…wouldn't she be foolish not to let her sister and brother-in-law lend a hand, just to give her breathing room? Thomas was right, in a way. If she took a short break from life, she might be able to function more efficiently and figure out what she was going to do with her future.

Besides, she mused, there was a secret part of her that had always yearned to break loose. To do something totally without consideration for what was proper or frugal. Sometimes she envisioned all the passion in her life stored up inside of her, waiting for a chance to gush forth like champagne from an uncorked bottle. Had she let Gary become the cork in her bottle? And now that he was gone…what sort of life would she live? A drab, uninteresting one? Or one that was adventurous and promised her new horizons? She imagined the next ten years flashing by as quickly and unremarkably as the first decade of her adult life.

"I...I don't know," she said softly, blinking away a hot, prickly sensation behind her eyelids.

"Don't think about it," Thomas growled impatiently. "Just say yes, and I'll finalize the arrangements." His hand found hers and closed over it, warm and reassuring. "You won't regret it. I promise."

She was trembling and she didn't know why. Reluctance to be separated from her children for so long? She didn't think so. She knew they would be safe with Elly as an escort and deliriously happy with their grandparents.

No, something else brought on the tremors. Something else terrified her. She met Thomas's intense brown eyes and a shudder of realization raced through her. She *wanted* him to kiss her again. She *wanted* him to crush her in his massive arms and make her remember what it felt like to be a woman.

Was that what she feared? That he would do all these things and more if she flew away with him? Then the summer would end and she'd be left with mere memories...and a lonely life back in Connecticut where she'd started.

"Say yes," he said, so low the words were a barely audible rumble across her kitchen.

Diane looked up at the man who seemed to fill a good half of the room. His eyes were glistening obsidian, hard with determination. The muscles in his face had turned rigid. Taut ridges ran down the sides of his neck, into the starched, white collar of his shirt.

He was an incredibly strong man. She had felt the muscles of his chest and arms when he'd held her. She imagined he would have a wealth of thick, richly textured hair across his chest that would be delightful to play with.

Why in Heaven's name was she thinking about a man's body when she should be concentrating on her future!

Diane drew herself up in her chair. *Now or never...now or never,* a persistent voice whispered through her mind. *Take a chance. Grab the ring. Risk your heart. For once in your life, do what feels good!*

She couldn't make her voice work for a full two minutes. "All right," she said at last. "I'll go."

Three

There was more to packing Diane's children off to their grandparents than Thomas had anticipated. All three had minds of their own, and each had specific ideas as to which clothing was "cool," which favorite stuffed animals or toys they simply could not leave behind. In the end the three suitcases Diane had planned expanded to six. One each for clothing and a smaller one for beloved teddy bears, pillows and playthings.

Elly arrived the morning of the trip flushed with excitement, her blond ponytail swinging like a metronome in time to the music playing through the earphones of her portable tape player. As lively as she was, she was a responsible girl, and Diane trusted her implicitly.

"They are definitely going to exhaust my parents,"

she said, laughing, as she waved all four of them through the boarding gate later that morning.

"I expect so," Thomas agreed, although he hadn't had much experience with youngsters.

In his view, children were a loud, frequently sticky, inexperienced tribe that interfered with an ordered adult life. You couldn't discuss politics with them without their eyes glazing over. You couldn't brawl with them the way you could with your mates on a football field. You couldn't talk about sex or Verdi or high-caliber weapons in their presence without generating scowls from other adults in the room. Children didn't seem of much use to him.

Yet Thomas had grown surprisingly fond of Jacob and Allison's babies. Cray was now three years old and called him Toms. The child just couldn't seem to get his mouth around that second syllable. Kristina was a delicate, squirming creature of six months. Thomas had been terrified of her at first. He was convinced that touching her with his big, awkward hands would instantly crush the child. But one day Allison simply plopped the baby in his arms as she took off across the garden after a runaway Cray. And there they'd been—the two of them. Thomas and Kristina. Staring at each other.

Thomas had instantly lost his heart to the blue-eyed mistress of the nursery.

Now he found excuses to hold her, to spend a few minutes of every day in the nursery soaking up the smell of talc and baby sweetness. He was convinced that little Kristina saved one special gurgle that sounded like ta-ta just for him. And she did something special for him whenever he held her. She relieved some of the torment he felt every time he looked in a mirror and saw his mother's face looking back at him. His mother, who had deserted him. He had always been convinced they were alike in ways other than physical, that he was as incapable of strong attachments as his mother had proved to be. But when he held little Kristina, he believed he might be a gentler, kinder, better person. For just those few minutes...the doubts and agonizing guilt went away.

But surely, these two royal children were different from all others. Diane's boisterous threesome were small strangers to him and likely to remain so. He told himself he was just doing what was necessary to help the prince's sister-in-law out of a jam. That was all.

No, he thought with sudden, grim clarity as he walked beside Diane through the terminal. There's more to it than that.

There was this maddening attraction that even now plagued him with prickly urgency to touch her as they walked through the terminal crowded with travelers. He remembered their kiss. He ached to repeat it. The thought of his lips on hers brought a sudden rush of heat to the nether regions of his body, and now a needy groan escaped his lips before he could stop it.

"Anything wrong?" Diane asked placidly, looking around at the busy airport shops with interest. Her eyes were a vivid, excited emerald today, full of anticipation of the adventure ahead. She seemed totally unaware of his torment.

"No. Nothing," he grumbled. He wistfully eyed a crowded bar to their right called Port of Call. A double scotch would take the edge off. But he was driving and couldn't indulge himself.

"It's too bad the flights couldn't have been closer

together,'' she mused, stopping to finger a pretty Irish wool shawl at an import shop. ''We might have been able to leave directly after putting the children on their plane instead of having to drive back to Nanticoke.''

''I had thought about that,'' he admitted. ''But there was a delay in completing the maintenance check, then new flight plans had to be filed. Your passport won't be delivered until later this afternoon. Seven hours' wait in an airport would be a bore.'' On the other hand, even an hour alone with Diane at the little Cape Cod wasn't likely to be relaxing. He felt wound tighter than Big Ben's spring.

''I suppose.'' She sighed. ''It's just as well. I still have some cleaning to do before I can lock up the house for the summer.'' She fell silent for the remainder of the hike to the short-term parking garage.

He wished he knew what she was thinking. Could she possibly guess how alert his body was to every move she made? The subtle sway of her full hips was enough to send sweat trickling down his spine under his clean white dress shirt. The purposeful tilt of her chin made his heart hammer. She seemed driven by a fresh supply of energy today—and he could think of dozens of ways to help her expend it.

Until now the children's presence and obstreperous enthusiasm for the trip had made it impossible for any real sense of intimacy to develop between them. Diane had been busy with laundry and packing, and he'd needed to verify the children's travel arrangements, then secure a car and driver to whisk the foursome directly from the arrival gate in Orlando to the grandparents' home.

The night before they were all to leave, ten o'clock

had rolled around before Diane had been able to get all three children settled in their beds. This admittedly had been an awkward time for him. Thomas had felt a restlessness growing inside as he'd contemplated their being alone at last. He hadn't realized how much he'd longed for a chance to have Diane to himself.

But before he'd been able to decide how best to handle the situation, Diane had announced she was "totally done in" and would be calling it a night. She'd handed Thomas a pillow and blanket, then nodded toward the couch. Disappointed, he'd stretched out on the lumpy cushions. Minutes passed. He'd thought about Diane lying in her bed in the other room. Tried to ignore the insistent cravings of his body. It had seemed impossible to find a comfortable position for his long body on the too-short sofa. He'd listened to the softly seductive sounds of Diane turning restlessly between her sheets, to her sighs as she drifted off to sleep...to his own heart racing in his chest. He hadn't slept at all.

But now an empty house awaited them. Thomas didn't know how he was going to keep his hands off Diane. If he'd been a religious man, he'd have prayed all the way from Long Island to Nanticoke. Instead, he concentrated on driving.

The traffic on I-95 was relatively heavy for a Sunday morning. He expected that was due to the season. During the summer, vacationers would be on the road and locals on their way to the beaches. Whatever the reason, he felt deeply grateful for the distraction the weaving cars and speeding RVs provided. He didn't have time to dwell on the hunger building inside his body.

As soon as he pulled the sedan into her driveway,

before his hands even left the steering wheel, Diane threw open the passenger door and bounded toward the house like an Olympic sprinter. He followed her inside, wondering why she was in such a rush. When he walked through the kitchen door, she was already on the telephone, speaking in regretful tones to the only child's mother she hadn't been able to reach the day before.

Thomas pressed the heels of his hands down on the back of a kitchen chair and waited until she finished giving the woman the name of two other day-care providers in town and hung up. "Was she giving you a hard time about leaving for the summer?"

Diane jumped as if she hadn't realized he was in the room. "Oh...not really. It's unsettling for a parent to have to alter child-care arrangements on short notice. The problem is, she may be so happy with one of the women I've recommended, I might not get her back in the fall."

"Perhaps you'll decide to choose another kind of job by the time you return."

"I know. I've been thinking a lot about alternatives."

Thomas couldn't seem to drag his eyes away from that expressive mouth of hers as she bubbled on about careers she'd once dreamed of having—a translator for the U.N., liaison for a diplomatic mission, member of a negotiating team on assignment in a foreign country. He didn't for a moment doubt she'd be good at any of them. But since she'd never had a job outside of her home, he feared she would need some time to work herself up the governmental ladder. Her lips twitched with emotion when she spoke, settled into a firm line of determination, pouted, trembled subtly, then lifted on a strand of hope. They were constantly moving. He longed to press his mouth over them, quiet them. Force them to respond to his own lips.

Diane laughed. "You aren't hearing any of this, are you?"

"Hmm?" He hastily brought his eyes up to meet hers. "Actually, I was listening. It's just that I was wondering—" He was wondering what she would taste like. Her lips…the soft valley between her breasts…her nipples…her honeyed thighs. "—just wondering why you never took a job in New York City or even Hartford. You could have made a lot more money working for a large corporation or the Federal government."

"Mostly I didn't want a career to eat up all my time and energy. The kids were more important to me." Diane swung around so quickly he was sure the maneuver was calculated to keep him from questioning her further. He stood as rigid as one of the sixteenth-century sculptures at the entrance to the palace garden as she swept out of the room. Her footsteps padded across the living room, then faded toward the far end of the house.

Thomas gripped the chair back all the harder. If he let go, he'd be tempted to follow her into her bedroom. An absurd and totally inappropriate impulse, he knew. Dangerous, he warned himself. Very, very dangerous, Thomas. Don't even think about it.

But through the thin walls, he could hear her moving about, rummaging in bureau drawers, tossing something that sounded clinky, like metal bracelets, onto her bed. Humming to herself.

He lowered his head and gritted his teeth. "No." He ground out the word. "*No,* you are *not* going anywhere near that woman!'' He counted to ten, tried it again, but only reached five before he was cut short by a loud thud followed immediately by a scream of pain.

Thomas bolted through the living room and ducked into the hallway that led to the bedrooms. ''Diane, are you all right?'' His heart pounding in his chest, he stopped in front of the first door on his left. From behind it came moaning sounds. He twisted the knob and rushed into the room.

She was sitting on the floor in very provocative underwear.

Thomas told himself he should get out, fast! But before he could move, Diane whipped her robe from the edge of the bed and threw it around herself.

Unfortunately, that didn't stop him from saving the image of her he'd seen. Thomas closed his eyes against the delicious vision and only then remembered his reason for bursting into her bedroom.

''Are you hurt?'' he whispered hoarsely.

''No, I'm just lounging around on the floor half-naked, holding my foot for the fun of it.'' A tear rolled down her flushed cheek.

He forced himself to look away for an instant, which was long enough to take in the rest of the room and sum up the situation. An enormous, hard-sided suitcase had fallen off the bed. ''You dropped that thing on your foot?''

She nodded.

He swore under his breath. ''You should have called me to move it for you if it was in your way.''

''I had already started to change clothes and I— Oh, wow, this really hurts.'' She winced and gripped her foot tighter. The tender flesh of her instep looked as if it was beginning to swell.

He shook his head, irritated with himself for reacting to the situation so slowly. "Hold on, I'll get some ice."

A minute later Thomas dashed back into her bedroom holding a plastic bag filled with ice cubes, a kitchen towel draped over his arm. She had somehow moved herself onto the bed, slipped her arms into her robe and securely knotted the tie around her waist. Her injured foot was propped on a pillow.

Even suffering, she was a stunning woman. The clothes she wore every day might be practical and inexpensive, her lifestyle simple and home centered...but underneath it all there was a woman of beauty and intelligence to rival any Continental socialite. He wanted her at that moment more than he'd ever wanted another.

"I should probably just stick my whole foot in a bucket of ice water," Diane said, gazing up at him with a vulnerable expression that melted his heart.

"No, this is more effective." He sat facing her on the bed. Gently he transferred her foot to the folded towel, then laid both on his thigh. Taking a single cube from the bag, he placed it against the puffy inner curve of her foot and started sliding it in small circles over the skin. "Tell me if this becomes too cold or if I hurt you," he said.

She nodded.

The ice massage did wonders for cooling down the inflammation. He stopped after ten minutes to inspect the tender skin, prodding it softly with his long fingers. "Nothing seems to be broken. And I doubt you've sprained it, since no twisting motion was involved. The weight of the luggage was probably enough to bruise you pretty badly, though. Can you stand on it?'' He looked up at her for the first time since he'd sat on the bed. Her eyes were a liquid-gold, shot through with emerald sparks.

''I think so.'' Diane's whisper was low and husky as she shifted her gaze to the wide hands wrapped around her foot. Rich-chestnut strands of hair fell across her face, only partially hiding the telltale flush of her cheeks.

He had kept his thoughts focused on treating her injury until now. Suddenly it was impossible for him to ignore the electric currents flashing between them. His lower body tightened; a sharp and sudden rush of heat coursed through his groin as their gazes locked. He'd been the object of *that look* from other women. It meant only one thing. And he'd never hesitated to take action.

This time must be different, he told himself firmly. No matter how fiercely his body urged him to respond to the invitation in her lovely eyes, he didn't dare surrender. The consequences for both of them would be disastrous.

Thomas hastily lifted her foot away from his thigh and stood beside the bed. ''Come on, let's see if you can walk,'' he said gruffly. ''If not, we may need to have a doctor look at it.''

Diane stared up at him bleakly. All the life seemed to drain from her face. The rosy tint fled her cheeks and brow, leaving her face as fragile and pale as egg-shell porcelain. With quiet grace, she stood up beside the bed. Gingerly at first she put a little weight on the injured foot. Then a little more. ''I think it's okay,'' she murmured.

"Good. Wear sensible shoes for a few days. No spike heels for Mother Fields." He grinned, trying to coax a smile out of her and lighten the tension between them. Instead, he was met by an icy glare.

"You think that's very funny, don't you?" she snapped, her body stiffening with anger.

He was at a loss. What had he said wrong? A moment ago she'd been weak with pain. Then she'd given him a clear signal that she would welcome an intimate follow-up to his bedside manner. And now the woman was balling up her fists in front of her as if she might actually come at him swinging! "What did I—"

"I'm not *your* kind of woman, is that the message you're trying to get across, Thomas? You can't imagine Diane Fields in a slinky, black, nothing-of-a-dress, wearing five-inch heels, diamonds dangling from her earlobes. Is that it?" She hobbled closer to him, her eyes flashing threateningly. "Why did you kiss me yesterday? You obviously aren't attracted to me. Was it a pity kiss? Were you under Jacob's orders to take my mind off my troubles?"

She turned her back to him but not before he saw the pained expression in her eyes.

"No!" he protested. "I only meant—" He took a hesitant step toward her.

She flipped a hand at him, warning him off without bothering to look back. "Never mind," she rasped. "I understand. No woman with a houseful of kids, an empty bank account and a department store wardrobe would ever interest a sophisticated bachelor like you." Her shoulders started to tremble, and her voice dropped to a near whisper. "Lately I'm not sure what *any* man sees when he looks at me. Obviously, I'm no longer terribly alluring.''

Her anguished words sank into his heart like pebbles dropped into a still pool. Ripples of amazement spread through him. How could this woman, whose mere presence in the same room inflicted such chaos on his insides, possibly think of herself as unattractive?

''It's not that,'' he said woodenly. But he couldn't explain the dozens of reasons keeping him from becoming involved with her—none of which had anything remotely to do with how she looked, smelled or felt in his arms. Even now, he was taunted by the bedroom lights playing off her rich-brown hair, the stubborn tilt of her narrow shoulders, the elusive fullness of her hips beneath her robe. It would be so easy to lay her down and divest her of that silly pink poof of a robe that was the only thing standing between him and the pleasures of her sweet body. Honest explanations were impossible.

His best diplomatic voice came to his rescue. ''I am the king's emissary and friend. I'm just trying to do my job and help your family. I never meant to upset you.''

She spun about to face him, and the anguish reflected in her eyes nearly destroyed him.

''Go. Leave me alone.'' Her voice was little more than a hoarse whisper. ''I want to take a nap before the flight. It's been a long two days.''

''Of course,'' he acquiesced.

A long two days. Her words echoed through his mind as he gently closed the bedroom door behind him. And tonight will be the longest of nights, he thought grimly. The two of them, confined to the intimate passenger cabin of Jacob's private jet. With no company for the eight-hour flight except their unfulfilled desires.

Thomas decided that now was an excellent time for a cold shower. A very long one.

By 6:00 p.m. they were on their way to the airport. Diane had slept fitfully for almost two hours, then stayed in her room, unwilling to face Thomas until she had sufficiently leashed her emotions. She hadn't felt at all hungry, hadn't ventured out to the kitchen to fix herself even a cup of tea. At one point she heard Thomas clattering around out there and soon smelled eggs and sausage cooking—the last of the food in the house. But when he'd tapped lightly on her door and asked if she wanted any, she hadn't answered him, and he'd eventually gone away.

Neither had spoken since.

She was no longer angry with Thomas, but his rejection hurt terribly. She felt ashamed for having lashed out at him. What had gotten into her? In a way, she supposed, the whole embarrassing scene might be her fault; she'd put him in an awkward position. She hadn't exactly begged him to sleep with her, but her body, with or without her permission, had been broadcasting seductive signals to him.

As he'd massaged her foot, his palm cupping each ice cube until it slowly melted into the towel beneath her heel, she'd felt heat, not cold, travel through her body. His hands were strong, warm and reassuring. A lover's hands. She visualized them traveling slowly up her leg, lifting away the hem of her robe, smoothing up her thigh...and touching her.

She'd thought she would evaporate into a puff of

frustrated steam when he abruptly stood up from the bed and looked down at her with that stiff British countenance of his. His eyes dark, glistening coldly. No sign of the passion she'd glimpsed, or thought she'd glimpsed, moments earlier when he'd rushed into her bedroom. He'd probably felt compelled to use his employment by the royal household as an excuse for not having sex with her. It was as convenient a way out as any.

Now Diane stared out the car window, pushing the troubling thoughts away as Thomas slowed the Benz to approach an airport gate at the area accommodating smaller, private planes. It was manned by a uniformed guard who waved the vehicle through. The Benz rolled to an effortless stop on a strip of tarmac between a hangar and a sleek silver jet embossed with the crimson emblem representing the monarchy of Elbia. Both metal and asphalt glowed red from the slanting rays of the setting sun. It seemed to her the entire Earth was being consumed by flames, and she with it.

As soon as they stopped, Thomas stepped quickly from the driver's seat and rounded the car to open her door for her. He took her arm and led her across the ruby-black landing apron toward the plane. Her foot still felt tender, but she could walk on it without real pain. A customs officer was waiting for them. He gave her luggage a cursory check, then stamped her new passport.

Introductions to the pilot and copilot were brief. Thomas showed her to her seat, which was a butter-soft wedge of leather couch, long enough to accommodate two people. She listened halfheartedly to

Thomas's polite offer of a drink or snack, but declined any refreshments with a stiff shake of her head.

He was being nice to her, but she still felt unwanted. Many other men, she suspected, would react exactly as he had, even without an employer's wrath to worry about. She just wasn't attractive enough to be worth the effort. Never in her life had she felt so humiliated, so alone and unloved. The ache in her heart was close to unbearable.

As the plane took off with a powerful surge into the oncoming darkness, she gazed out the curved window at a purple- and rose-streaked sky and felt the sting of the day lessen just a little as the jet gained altitude. She decided she would use the flight time to put the pain behind her and look forward to seeing Allison and her little niece and nephew. If she could just focus on the happy things in her life, she would be okay. She would. She really would. To hell with men!

Diane shot a sideways glance at Thomas buckled into a seat across the aisle. He was punching the keys of a laptop computer, hunt-and-peck style, scowling intently at the screen. If he punched any harder, she mused, his index fingers would shoot straight through the machine into his kneecaps. It gave her a small amount of satisfaction to know he was upset, too. Though why he should be, she had no idea. He'd been the one to set the rules.

For the first hour of the flight, Diane pretended to read the paperback novel she'd brought from home. But she became aware of Thomas stealing glances her way, then observing her for longer periods of time, the laptop idle beneath his fingers. At last she closed the book and turned to look at him across the empty expanse of leather between them.

"What is it?" she asked.

His dark eyes glistened solemnly. "I'm sorry," he said tightly. "I've hurt your feelings."

She lifted her chin with dignified grace. "I'll survive."

"I want to make up for it." He hesitated. "Just tell me what I must do. Please."

Diane laughed. She couldn't help it. Suddenly she felt so emotionally drained she was incapable of being anything but absolutely candid about what had happened between them. "I realize I'm not a very glamorous woman," she began. "But I had hoped that, just once, just—" She looked forward to the half-closed sliding partition that separated the luxurious ten-seat passenger compartment from the cockpit. She could see the back of the pilot's seat and the glowing dials on the control panel beyond him.

Thomas set the laptop aside, unclasped his seat belt and quickly moved to fully close the door between the cabin and cockpit. Instead of returning to his own seat, he settled on the leather bench beside her, then leaned so close to her she felt his warm breath against her cheek when he spoke. "Go on, they can't hear now."

She wasn't sure why she felt the need to explain herself to the Englishman, of all people. But something inside of her demanded she put into words some of the feelings she'd kept locked away in her heart for so very long. Never had she confided her most intimate secret even to her own sister. And she would never, never reveal *that* to any man! But perhaps she could reveal a small corner of her heart, to ease her own loneliness.

"It sounds awful," she began slowly. "I'm not that kind of woman. But I suppose I was hoping for a...um, for a one-night stand."

Thomas grimaced, looking puzzled. "Why would you want to do that?" he asked. "To get back at your husband for deserting you?"

"No!" She shook her head violently. Revenge wasn't her way of dealing with people who hurt her. "No," she repeated more softly. "I guess I just wanted to find out what passion, *real* passion uncomplicated by other emotions felt like...even if it lasted no longer than a few hours."

Thomas stared at her, his eyes deepening nearly to black. He raked a hand through the thick, dark-brown hair over his forehead. "That husband of yours was a bloody fool," he rumbled low in his throat. "A fellow just has to look at you to see you're more woman than most men could handle."

Her heart abruptly ceased beating, missed several pulses, then picked up its rhythm double-time. Diane narrowed her eyes at him, suspicious of his unexpected compliment. Or was he just teasing her? "Is this you talking, Thomas...or the result of another directive from Jacob?"

His hand moved so fast she barely saw it and didn't have a chance to pull away. He seized her arm and gave her a good, hard shake. "Look at this face, woman!" he demanded in a harsh whisper. "Do you see a man blindly following orders?"

She gazed up at him, shaken by the startling change in his manner, searching his tormented features for meaning. A dangerous hunger seethed in his eyes, tugged at the muscles beneath his jaw, sent a shiver of fear through her.

"No." She choked out the word. "No, not now. I don't think what Jacob wants is on your mind."

"Damn right. If I hadn't believed I was betraying Jacob's trust," he hissed at her, "I swear I'd have thrown you down on that bed so fast—"

"You mean I...I excite you?" Diane stared at him, forgetting to be frightened. She was honestly amazed. She felt like a child waking from a dream, unable to differentiate between the last traces of fantasy and a slowly emerging real world.

"Excite me?" he bellowed. "Woman, you drive me out of my mind and very nearly out of my pants!"

Diane clapped a hand over his mouth, laughing in spite of her embarrassment. "Hush." She nodded toward the front of the plane. That partition didn't look nearly solid enough to be soundproof.

He pulled her fingertips from his lips and kissed them softly before folding them within his hand on the cushion between them. His gaze skipped around the plush, mahogany-paneled compartment as if seeking a safer resting place than on any part of her.

At last he met her curious eyes. "From the moment I met you," he began cautiously, "I wondered how you might look with your clothes off. Does that shock you?"

She quickly shook her head, then grinned. "Maybe a little."

"I thought about what it would feel like to take you away somewhere. Somewhere we could be alone together, just the two of us. Jacob's yacht...an island...the chateau I bought two summers ago in Switzerland. After a while, it didn't matter where. And you can take my word for it, when you crossed my mind it was purely as a woman...and with a great deal of shame and frustration because you were married and had a family. I couldn't lay a damn finger on you!''

She took a long time to digest his delicious confession. He'd hidden his attraction to her so well, she never would have guessed it existed.

''When you...when you kissed me yesterday,'' she began tentatively, then shook her head in frustration because the words came out so awkwardly, ''I thought it was because you felt sorry for me.''

He rolled his eyes toward the low ceiling of the compartment. ''I kissed you, woman, because I didn't have the strength *not* to kiss you.'' He spoke slowly, carefully now, as if it was important to him that she understand. Despite his calm exterior, she was aware of enormous tension building within his fingers, hands, traveling up his arms and tightening his shoulders as he reached for and captured her other trembling hand. His gaze locked with hers. ''I barely had the self-control to stop at just a kiss. I wanted to ravage you, head-to-toe.''

She blinked twice, three times, her heart racing...ran her tongue between dry lips. No man had ever spoken such words to her. Such amazing words. At last she found the courage to whisper the thought echoing through her heart.

''What?'' he asked leaning closer.

This time she didn't blink. ''I said, 'If it happens again...*don't* stop.' ''

Thomas swallowed audibly. ''You have no idea what you're asking of me, Diane.'' He drew a long, shaky breath, then let it out gradually. For the first time since he'd moved to her side of the plane, he allowed his gaze to drop to the soft swells shaped by her breasts within her striped cotton tunic. His hand strayed upward. With curved knuckles he lightly brushed the side of her left breast, as if he was testing his own willpower as well as her invitation.

"What if Jacob found out?" he breathed, watching his finger trace the outline of her bra through the fabric. "What if I slept with you, but you later regretted it?"

"I wouldn't tell him, and I would never regret making love with you." But she immediately wondered if she really knew how she would feel after having sex with a man she barely knew.

"What if you were disappointed?"

She giggled. *He* was worried about disappointing *her?* "I would have thought your male ego would have assured you that's impossible."

He shook his head. "You're different from the other women who have passed through my life. Better," he added hastily, when her expression must have warned him he had crossed an invisible line and was close to upsetting her again. "They all—" he searched for the right words, lifted his hand and pressed his palm tenderly to her cheek "—they were accustomed to playing intimate games with men, without ever becoming truly intimate. I doubt any of my lovers gave one ounce of her soul to me. And I know I never gave mine to them."

His words were beautiful, but he still hadn't said they would sleep together. Rejection, even for logical reasons, still felt like rejection. "You're saying," she began hesitantly, "that you don't believe I could make love to a man without falling in love with him?''

Thomas brushed an errant wave of dark hair from over her eyes. "Exactly. And I don't want to find myself in the position of being the one to hurt you."

"I'm not like that," she stated with more confidence than she felt.

"You don't want a fling," he insisted. "You need a real man, one who will stand by you. Deep down, Diane, like any good woman…you want forever."

Her cheeks burning with indignation, she glared at him. A lump threatened to close her throat, but she forced bitter words over it. "What gives you the right to say what I want?" she demanded.

"You're too nice to—"

Diane huffed at him, pulling away. "I'm too nice to have sex with a man and enjoy it for its own sake? Is that what you're saying? Too good to have a torrid love affair just for the fun of it?" She glared at him. "Don't I have a right to even a little happiness after suffering through eight years of a cold, loveless marriage to a man who never once in our relationship made me—" She clamped her mouth shut, appalled by what she'd nearly revealed—the secret that was so mortifying she'd vowed it would remain hers alone.

Thomas studied her for a long moment while she held her breath and itched uncomfortably in her seat, trying to avoid his piercing eyes, praying he hadn't been able to put the rest of the pieces together on his own. "Your husband never sexually satisfied you?" he asked diplomatically.

"I-I'm not sure." She slid as far away from him

on the seat as possible and looked frantically out the window at the black night sky.

"If you'd been there, dear girl, you would know it," Thomas stated.

Dear Lord, how would she ever be able to look the man in the eye again? He must think she was ridiculously naive! Probably even stupid. Yet she knew from sad experience that it was possible to go through the motions of the physical act that seemed so exciting and beautiful in novels and movies without feeling anything but frustration. There had been no joy with Gary. No soaring highs and no dazzling fireworks. No passion.

Thomas coughed as much to clear the air, she suspected, as his throat. "I'm sorry, that wasn't a very tactful thing to say. But it seems to me a bloody shame for a warm, lovely woman like you never to have had an orgasm."

She shrugged.

"On the other hand," he continued, still sounding angry, "if no man has ever made love to Diane Fields the right way, it's her partner's fault not hers." His long arm shot out and, despite the increased distance between them, he caught her chin between his thumb and forefinger and firmly guided her back to face him.

"Lovely lady, I could show you how it ought to be between a man and a woman. Teaching you would bring me the greatest pleasure." He stood up in front of her and smiled down softly, the outrage in his voice gone. He looked both intrigued and tempted by the prospect.

"But you can't...because of your loyalty to Jacob?"

"That's right."

Sensing he was about to return to his own seat, she impulsively decided she wasn't going to let him off that easily.

Diane reached up, gripped one of Thomas's strong hands and hauled him down beside her. Before he could recover his balance or composure, she quickly placed her arms around his neck, pressing her body against the solid wall of his muscled chest. She tilted her head back and parted her lips, feeling a shudder rip through his body as he sighed and took her mouth with all the hunger of a starving man.

Only then did she move away and settle back into the curve of smooth leather with a satisfied smile.

"I just wanted you to understand what you'd be missing," she murmured, closing her eyes to enjoy the delicious ripples of heat radiating through her. "I, for one, don't give a royal hoot what Jacob thinks."

Four

Diane stood at the window of the spacious bedroom she had been given in the castle. Below stretched a walled garden, its paths outlined in neatly clipped hedges. Roses bloomed in lush abundance, mostly reds and pinks, but a few peach and white blossoms clustered around a stone garden bench. On that bench sat a man with trim, dark hair and a brooding countenance. He looked deeply disturbed by his secret thoughts.

Diane grinned. Good. That kiss over the Atlantic had given Thomas Smythe something to think about.

It wasn't that she meant to be cruel or a tease, she told herself. She liked him, really she did. But his refusal to give in to the same temptation that was frustrating her…well, that infuriated her.

She sighed and collapsed heavily on the cushioned windowseat. For a long time she had numbed herself to all feelings that might be called sensual, sexy or erotic. There had been so little time for that sort of thing. She'd been far too busy raising her children and running a home and business, and Gary preferred to spend his free time at the local watering hole.

Like a fine piano, neglected and left unplayed for months at a time, she had fallen out of tune with the romantic world. Adorably infatuated couples on TV, daring lovers in movies, stories of reckless passion in books all left her cold. She had no way of identifying with those model-perfect heroes and heroines who experienced life intensely and loved ardently. Did real people ever behave this way—wrapping their naked bodies around each other with moans of delight? Did real men and women suffer unquenchable yearnings for each other? Ford rushing rivers…scale mountains…challenge destiny to be together?

She had stopped believing such love existed until Allison and Jacob were reunited nearly three years after her sister conceived the young prince's child. Then she saw in their eyes a desire so compelling she couldn't ignore it. For the only time in her life she envied her sister. No, she didn't want Jacob. What she coveted was the joy of feeling like a woman, deep in her bones, right down to her soul.

She had never felt that.

Then she'd met Thomas, and desire had curled through her, reminding her there were reasons why women enjoyed the company of men.

Diane shivered as a warm, mysterious ribbon pulled slowly through her feminine core. She had been playing with fire when she teased Thomas on the plane. She'd known that, even as they'd kissed.

Yet she hadn't been able to stop herself. What sort of sense did that make?

She looked down into the garden again. To her horror she found Thomas had left the bench and was standing immediately below her window, looking up at her. She froze, met his dark eyes, couldn't look away. Her palms grew moist; her mouth went dry. Her entire body prickled with anticipation as his gaze hardened, held hers. If she'd had any doubt whether or not he wanted her, it was gone now. But she remembered his words on the plane. He wouldn't do anything to dishonor Jacob.

Damn him.

Damn the two of them.

"Are you awake?" a familiar voice called from the doorway behind her.

"Yes," Diane breathed.

She heard Allison approach, but didn't turn away from the window. Not until Thomas lowered his eyes and disappeared beneath the rose-blanketed stone arch leading into the lower level of the castle. Roses were nice, but they couldn't hold her interest after the fervor of the Englishman's gaze.

Diane faced her sister. "Just admiring your garden."

Wrapping her arms around her, Allison hugged hard. "It's so good to see you. I wish you'd been able to come to us sooner."

"You know how it is—the kids have school, and I have the day-care business. It's hard to find coverage for even one day, let alone a week or two."

"But you're here now and we'll spend the summer together!" Allison said joyfully.

She had always been the more delicate of the two

sisters. Her skin was nearly translucent, while Diane's was tanned golden by the sun. Allison's hair was a shimmering blond, smooth, falling down her back in a fine veil. A distinct contrast to Diane's dark brown pageboy. She was a few inches shorter than Diane and of a lighter bone structure. But they'd always been close in matters of the heart.

Diane nodded. Yes, if she could just put aside forbidden emotions, they would have fun together. And she would luxuriate in the rare freedom of not being in charge of a gaggle of lively youngsters. She adored her kids, but she had called her parents as soon as she'd arrived and they assured her that the children were having the time of their lives. So now, for once, it was her time. Time to indulge herself. "What do we do first?" she asked.

"Actually, we have some time to think about that," Allison stated, sounding apologetic. "I have several meetings that were scheduled months ago, and I can't miss them. They involve our Children's Rescue League."

"I understand. Of course you must go," Diane agreed. "I'll be fine on my own until you're free."

"You won't have to be on your own." Allison's blue eyes sparkled merrily.

"I won't?"

"No. I spoke with Thomas this morning and asked him to show you around the city."

A minor chord twanged in Diane's heart. So that was why he had looked so upset. He had been contemplating having to spend the day with her. Either he hadn't liked the idea at all, or he'd liked it far too much for what he deemed his own good. Diane hid a smile behind her hand and felt just a teensy bit wicked. How far did she dare go?

A flash of his large hands against the bruised skin of her foot teased her mind. Warmed her from inside. She would love to know what those marvelous fingers would feel like on other parts of her body.

She became aware that Allison was still talking, and she hastily refocused her thoughts to listen to the tail end of a list of nearby tourist sites. "I have to rush off for now." Her sister moved toward the door. "But I'll be back tonight for dinner, as will Jacob. We'll chat about plans for your vacation then."

"That's fine," Diane assured her.

"Thomas will take good care of you." Allison gave her one last reassuring wink, then was gone, leaving behind a whisper of her perfume—lilacs and sweet william.

Diane decided the outcome of the day was out of her hands. It would either be the best of any in recent times, or the very worst. She supposed that would depend upon Thomas.

By eleven o'clock that morning, her private tour of the fifteenth-century castle had already taken nearly two hours, even though Thomas moved at an aerobics-class pace. He hadn't slowed as he'd pointed out a Tintoretto oil on one wall, then a breathtaking Velázquez followed by a solemn Dürer. All of the paintings were magnificent, as were the sculptures that waited to surprise her in the least expected turns and niches in the long corridors. The marble of David—nude, glorious in his determination, beautifully muscled—left her weak in the knees and was her favorite. But Thomas swept her on, past tapestries of unicorns, medieval battles and exquisitely gowned ladies. He spouted historical details about the victories and defeats of the various residents of Der Kristallenpalast, the crystal palace, as the fortress at Elbia had been known for centuries, because of the shimmering appearance of its rare, quartz-streaked, white Russian marble. He barely took a breath between facts. And he always, always kept a safe distance of several feet between himself and her.

At first Diane was amused and flattered by his anxiety. But by the time they left the castle proper and crossed the courtyard to the royal stables, she'd grown irritated with his refusal to acknowledge the mounting sensual tension between them. When he courteously held a door for her as they entered the low cedar-lined building, she sensed his free hand hovering behind her back as if to guide her through. On a perverse whim, she stopped dead in the doorway.

Thomas's hand kept moving and settled briefly in the curve of her spine. She turned to face him, but he quickly jerked his hand away and started to step back.

"Don't you dare run away." She flashed her eyes up at him.

He stopped where he was and stared at her in open-mouthed confusion.

"And don't pretend you have no idea what's been going on all morning," she scolded, catching his wayward brown eyes with hers and holding them.

A groom passed by them, and she could sense Thomas's body tightening another notch. "Nothing is going on," he said firmly.

"Oh, no? Thomas, you were practically galloping through the castle. If you don't want to play host, just say so. I'll find my own way around and probably have a better time. At least I won't pass out from exhaustion.''

''I'm sorry if I was walking too fast for you, Mrs. Fields,'' he said loudly enough to be heard by anyone in the stable.

''Thomas-s-s-s,'' she hissed at him, ''cut it out.'' She leveled a glare at him she usually reserved for a disobedient child.

Backing into a wooden pillar, he let his shoulders slump as he leaned against it for support. ''It's that obvious…what I'm thinking?''

''Yes.''

''I will try to control myself better.''

''That's not what I want.''

He looked at her warily. ''I already told you…we can't—''

''I want for us to be friends,'' she said. ''I like you, Thomas, you know that. I want to stop pretending and just act like two adults who are attracted to each other but have agreed nothing can happen beyond friendship.''

He stared at her, and she wondered what he was thinking.

''Don't you think that's possible?'' she asked.

''I'm not accustomed to—'' He looked away from her, a shadow crossing his perplexed features. ''When I'm attracted to a woman, I usually find a way to…to be with her. If not right away, sometime later.''

''Later, when Jacob doesn't require your services?''

''Yes.''

She nodded slowly. ''And what if she says she's not interested?''

A flicker of a grin passed over his full lips, and he

turned back to her. "That hasn't happened in recent memory."

A chill raced through her. An exceedingly pleasant, very urgent chill. What would it be like to be with such a man? A man who knew how to please a woman, just for mutual delight? No attachments. No promises. The two of them sharing a physical moment.

Diane thought about the long, busy years since college. She'd been a good woman, dedicated to her children, hardworking, faithful to a husband who didn't love her. Didn't she deserve one summer fling in her lifetime?

And it wasn't as if Thomas was just any man she'd picked up on a beach or in a bar. She liked him immensely, and he was, she felt sure, a kind man. A man who wouldn't hurt her. A man who would take care of her pleasure as thoroughly as he'd see to his own.

The thought of their being together began to simmer inside of her. But how did a woman convince a man to put aside what he viewed as his honor, just for a little while, to make love to her?

In novels, the heroine seduced her man. She batted her eyes at him, slithered close, tossed her head provocatively, bared cleavage. Me? she thought, and nearly giggled.

"Thomas," she said quietly. "I know I'm not like the other women in your life. But you say you're attracted to me?"

He dropped his chin a bare inch then raised it again in agreement. His eyes darkened, the black pupils dilating perceptibly. She felt sure the delicate throbbing of the vein in his right temple intensified.

"I want to have an affair." That was as plain as she could make it.

He stared at her.

"But I don't want to have it with just anyone. I want him to be a friend. I want to have sex with a friend. Is that so obscene?"

"N-no," he finally found his voice. "But I don't believe you understand the consequences, in our case."

"And they are?"

"As I explained before, we must consider your family and my position. But there's also the difference between our natures. A man can have intimate relations with a woman and walk away from the bed feeling nothing more than grateful for a pleasant experience. A woman can't."

"You believe a woman has to fall in love with every man she sleeps with?"

"Not every woman." He was observing her so intently, she shuddered under the weight of his gaze.

"A woman like me."

"Yes."

"Why do you think that?"

He opened his hands and slowly settled them on her shoulders. "Because you are a moral woman, Diane. You aren't accustomed to meaningless affairs. You would be hurt when it was over. I couldn't do that to you."

"Don't you think I should have a choice in the matter?"

"Not if it's the *wrong* choice." His voice suddenly held a brittle edge. His eyes turned to black flames. "Don't be foolish, woman."

She slapped him across the face.

For a moment Diane felt as stunned as he looked. Never in her life had she raised a hand against another person—adult or child. She'd just struck Thomas, when all he'd done to deserve it was tell her he wished to do the honorable thing.

"I-I'm so sorry." His cheek was turning pink where the flat of her hand had landed. She gently pressed her palm to the inflamed skin. "I didn't mean to— Oh, Thomas. It's just that you can't know what's best for me when—"

He moved so quickly she didn't have time to finish her apology. With a quick glance down the straw-covered alley, he dragged her into an empty stall and latched both top and bottom halves of the split door. The space smelled of cedar, sweet clean straw and horseflesh.

Thomas pressed her against the plank wall and dove for her mouth with bruising intention. He forced her lips open, swept his tongue over the sharp edges of her teeth then deeper. He tasted of coffee with a touch of scotch, and she thought fleetingly that he must have fortified himself for their tour after Allison gave him his assignment.

"Is this what you want?" he demanded, bending to roughly kiss her throat. He was so much taller than she, he had to contort his body to reach her. Then he was lifting her with ease to his level, raking his lips the length of her throat, down into the collar of her shirt.

What *did* she want? To be ravaged in a stable? No. Or maybe, yes. Maybe that would make her feel alive again. It had been so long, so very long since she'd felt wanted. As harsh as Thomas was trying to be,

Diane was more curious than afraid of him. His left hand found her breast, and while he still pinned her between the wall of his chest and wall of wood, he kneaded the sensitive flesh through the fabric of her shirt. If he intended to shock her, he failed. His big hand felt glorious, and she wanted more.

"You're not going to scare me off," she gasped.

"Dangerous," he growled between kisses. "Too dangerous."

Yes, in the stable where a groom might wander in at any time, they were taking a risk. Or was he talking about something else, another sort of peril?

But even as he was warning both of them, his hands were doing remarkable things to her body. They traveled beneath her blouse and bra, kneading her throbbing breasts, caressing her nipples to erection with his thumbs. They smoothed down over her skirt, lifted its hem, shot upward along her thighs. When he pressed her hips against his taut, muscled thighs, she felt his arousal, hard and long beneath the zipper of his trousers, against her stomach. She wondered if he was as generously sized there as the rest of his body. The thought sent delicious chills through her.

Diane closed her eyes as he reached between her thighs. His fingers slid expertly beneath the elastic of her panties. Even before he touched the tender folds of flesh, swollen with heat, aching for him, she sensed a primal flow of moisture.

"One of us must stop this," he ground out in her ear.

"No," she whispered. "Not…yet."

His fingers felt hot and lightly callused and strong as he stroked her. She arched against him, pressing her back against the unyielding boards. Her heart pounded wickedly, urgently against her ribs. When she opened her eyes, they failed to focus. All she could see was a blur of dark hair, a wall of chest, a tower of man—then he was kissing her again, his fingers moving more urgently, cleverly, finding the most sensitive places, transporting her so high she could only throw her arms around his strong neck, cling to him, let him take her wherever he chose. And hope she survived the fall when he released her. She still wanted more.

Instinctively Diane reached down and grasped his wrist. Their eyes met in understanding. She wasn't pushing him away; it was a plea. He thrust his fingers deeper, and she pressed herself against his curled knuckles, feeling her feminine muscles tighten around him, spasm delightfully, tighten again.

''Oh, my!'' she gasped between his lips.

It had been so long, so very, very long. And it had never been like this for her. Never. The fierceness of her response rocked her, and she had to reach up again and hold on to Thomas. He understood her hunger and kept time with her rhythms, stayed within her, sliding his two thick fingers in and out, bringing wave after wave of steamy ecstasy to her starved body as he pressed his mouth over hers to smother her cries of exultation.

A silver cloud closed around her, and she suddenly felt so very dizzy she knew she couldn't stand without support. All sense of time left her. Nothing existed but the pleasure he was giving her. A desperate need to see and touch him as he was touching her flashed across her subconscious. But in her mind Thomas's words echoed, *Dangerous...too dangerous.*

Besides, he was doing things to her that made it impossible for her to act. All strength, all volition deserted her. She could only submit as he brought her to yet another...and another climax. He was right. If she'd been here before, she would have known.

At last she rested her head back against the cedar planks, let her arms drop limply from his shoulders and drew a long shuddering breath. She felt spent, tingling. She closed her eyes and let the rest of the world settle back into place before she opened her eyes.

"Are you all right?" Thomas asked in his deepest rumble.

Diane looked dreamily up at him, her lips curving in a soft smile. "Never better. You?"

"Not so good, I'm afraid." He grimaced charmingly at her.

"We can do something about that," she suggested playfully.

"No." He tucked in his rumpled shirt, walked to the door and listened for a moment, raked his fingers through his hair and glowered at the spot on the dirt floor where they'd tramped down the straw.

"Thomas, we didn't do anything to hurt anyone."

"I've broken my trust," he muttered.

"You gave me immense pleasure," she whispered.

"I don't expect that's the sort of recreation the king and queen planned for you, do you?" He looked pointedly at her.

"Why should what they want be so important?" she asked tightly. "Why doesn't what you or I want count for anything?"

He shook his head. "You can't understand."

"No," she said tightly, "I guess I can't." She

stuffed her feet back into her leather flats, which had mysteriously come off her feet, and rebuttoned her blouse.

Blindly Diane raced out through the stable doors, across the yard, muttering to herself, but finding rich consolation in the knowledge that she'd left Thomas in dire need. "Serves the man right," she spat.

Thomas let loose with every British, German and American cuss word he knew. *What* had he been thinking? He'd started the day with the best intentions. Yes, he understood that Diane Fields wanted to have an affair with him. But he'd made it perfectly clear to the woman that this could never happen. There were so many reasons it was a bad idea. He'd gone over them repeatedly in his own mind and thought he'd given her a logical explanation, as well.

If she was determined to have sex with a man, let her go ahead and do it—but not with him. If they were discovered, his friendship with Jacob would forever be blackened. His job, which he loved, would likely be snatched away from him. But most of all, he feared the effect Diane had on him, which was unlike that of any other woman.

Never had he lost control as he had with her in the stables. Never had he gone against his own solemnly arrived-at intentions. But all she'd had to do was look up at him with those amazing hazel eyes of hers, and he'd thrown away the game plans.

By confronting him she had forced him to react to her when he'd intended to handle her tour of the castle and its grounds with utmost decor and civility. His only recourse had been to try to frighten her away. If he came at her like a bull, stopped treating her like the king's sister-in-law, she'd soon realize he wasn't what she wanted or needed. But it hadn't worked. Somewhere along the way, he'd stopped trying to protect her and selfishly pleased himself.

Now the thought of how brutally he'd manhandled her drove him mad. No, he hadn't seduced her, but he might as well have. The will had been there. He'd ached to throw her down on the stable floor and plunge into her. Seeing her surrender herself totally to him had been a powerful aphrodisiac. He shared her climaxes, challenged himself to take her ever higher.

How could he have done such a terrible thing?

Thomas took a very long walk to try to settle himself down.

When he at last returned by way of the garden gates, high-pitched squeals and laughter greeted him. He looked up from the stony path to see Allison with the little prince and princess. He couldn't face her now, not after what he'd just done.

Making a smart about-face, Thomas took the long way back to the castle.

By dinnertime that night, he still hadn't figured out how to deal with the issue of Diane. He knew he'd hurt her feelings by refusing to become her summer lover. But the circumstances were impossible, he told himself for the hundredth time. She was far better off suffering brief rejection, then returning to the States to find a man who would be a proper husband. He had no doubt that a woman with as much to offer as Diane would find eager suitors once it became clear she was available.

But that was, he suddenly realized, yet another

problem, for he found he didn't much like the idea of another man touching her as he had...or making love to her completely, as he hadn't.

The family met for dinner in the private dining parlor to one side of the smallest of the three kitchens. The formal dining room was enormous and used only for state occasions, while the parlor had a cozier feeling and accommodated only eight. He arrived later than the rest of the family. Allison and Diane were chatting animatedly about Diane's shopping trip in Elbia that afternoon. He hoped no one would ask why she'd had to go alone.

He tried to keep Jacob busy with conversation about the king's upcoming trip to Canada in hopes of shutting out the sweetly mesmerizing sound of Diane's voice. But sometime during dessert, Thomas overheard Allison react to something her sister had said.

"I really don't think it's a good idea," she said softly. "Elbia's night life is pretty tame when compared to Paris, London or Rome...but a place with the reputation of Zandoor's isn't appropriate for a woman on her own."

"Zandoor's?" Thomas repeated before he could stop himself.

Diane grinned at him. "A tourist guide told me the night club was very exciting—live music, lots of interesting people and good food."

"It's a pickup joint," Thomas said crisply.

"You see?" Allison said, looking relieved to have some support. "If you're intent on sampling the night life, you should go with a group."

"Or take Thomas," Jacob said with a casual wave

of his fork. "He's equal to any three men. I can personally vouch for that."

Diane slanted a meaningful look at Thomas and mouthed the words *Me, too.*

He shifted in his chair and turned quickly back to Jacob. "I promised you the agenda for Friday's meeting by tomorrow morning. I still need to do some work on it."

"The afternoon will be good enough."

Thomas nodded and lost what was left of his appetite. He pushed away his half-eaten slice of Linzertorte—the hazelnut, raspberry and spices he so loved, forgotten.

"I really don't need a chaperon," Diane insisted.

Thomas prayed Jacob would let that pass as a refusal of his company. But His Royal Highness had never taken no for an answer.

"If you still want to go," Jacob stated, "Thomas will drive you and be there, just in case you need him."

Zandoor's was throbbing with world-beat music. One minute tribal in rhythm, the next Irish, gypsy, Australian aboriginal or hopped-up American swing. It never stopped.

The club was crammed with lively dancing, talking, laughing people of all ages. Diane was excited. She couldn't remember the last time she'd gone clubbing and wished Allison could have come with her. But she understood her sister's responsibilities to her children and her royal image. Luckily, *she* wasn't royalty and could do as she pleased.

Thomas followed closely behind as Diane pushed herself through the crush of bodies in the main room, even though she'd asked him to stay in the car. He glowered at the gyrating couples on the dance floor as if any one of them might be a paid assassin in disguise.

"Have you been here before?" she shouted above the gut-thudding reverberations.

"Not my kind of place," he muttered.

"Not mine, either, but it looks like fun!" A man standing at the bar caught her eye, and she smiled back. She'd forgotten how much fun it was to flirt. "Get lost for a while, will you, Thomas? I don't want you frightening off prospects." She was only half teasing. She'd noticed more than a few intimidated expressions as she and her bodyguard passed by.

An hour later Diane finished her first martini and started on a second sent to her by a striking young man at a nearby table. She raised her glass to him in thanks. Before he could move to the seat beside her at the bar, another man asked her to dance. She felt the tiniest bit wild and gave herself to the loud music and heady beverages until the room began to spin gently. She danced some more, but prudently turned down a third martini from yet another stranger.

Meanwhile, Thomas lurked in a dark corner, observing her with a disapproving glare. She was glad he was angry. She'd laid her soul bare to him, and he'd turned her down! Although now she at least knew he wanted her, too. Diane gazed about the crowded, dark room, searching for someone she'd feel safe leaving with, just to put Thomas in his place. She would never sleep with a stranger, but Thomas didn't know that. Pretending she merely had to choose a partner for the night gave her a jolt of wicked satisfaction.

It was nearly midnight when Thomas finally broke. She was dancing with a man with sexy blue eyes and blond hair, who told her he was a skiing instructor. At least she thought that was what he'd said, since he spoke no English and her college German was rusty. They were dancing to one of the few slow songs the band had played that night and, as he brought her closer and she rested her head on his shoulder, she felt his hand wandering lower on her back, and her body tensed. His palm spread across her bottom and he gave her a too-friendly squeeze.

Before Diane could protest, she felt a violent jerk and her partner was gone. She looked around, mystified, and spotted a tall figure plowing through the crowd of dancers with a fragile-looking man struggling like a marionette from his huge fist.

"Thomas!" she cried. Oh, God, she thought, he's going to kill him.

What had she done?

Scrambling between bodies, she went after them. She caught up with Thomas and her former dance partner at the club's front door.

"Wait!" she gasped. "I'm sorry. This is all my fault."

"You wanted him to touch you like that?" Thomas roared.

"No, but I could have handled it myself."

The man was staring at Thomas in horror, then at her. "Ist er ihres Mann?"

"No, I'm not her husband!" Thomas barked, releasing him.

The man didn't wait for further explanations. He was through the door and into the street before Diane could apologize. The music in the room behind them grew louder and the beat intensified. She could hardly think. "Come outside!" she shouted up at Thomas, then took his hand and led him into the cool night air. Even in the dark she could see the white-tipped mountains surrounding Elbia. Moonlight splashed the shop-lined streets with a silvery glow.

She sat down on a bench and patted the spot beside her for Thomas. They remained silent for what seemed a very long time. The music from the club provided a distant backdrop of steady bass beats that echoed against the quaint, old buildings.

At last she sighed. "I can't stay in Elbia unless we come to some kind of agreement."

"I know," he returned gruffly.

"I can leave."

He shook his head. "You were right before when you said we should be able to be friends and acknowledge our attraction for each other. I wasn't being completely honest when I told you my only reasons for not wanting to start an affair with you were Jacob and you."

"Oh?"

"I'm forty years old. It must have occurred to you that there is a reason I haven't married."

"I thought your loyalty to Jacob…"

"He would never deny me a family," Thomas said quietly. "I choose not to marry for reasons of my own inadequacy."

Now she was really confused. "I don't understand."

"When I was not quite five years old, my mother left me, my two younger brothers and our father. She walked out of our lives, and to my knowledge she's never looked back. At least, I haven't seen her since."

"I'm so sorry," Diane breathed. She couldn't imagine any woman doing such a thing. She thought of her own children and felt faintly nauseous. How often had she worried about losing them to an accident or sickness? But to voluntarily leave them…

"My father," Thomas continued, "true to the nature of most British males, was not a warm, nurturing man. He saw to our physical needs, and we had a nanny, but as soon as each of us turned six, we were shipped off to boarding school. I only returned home on holidays."

Diane nodded. "I see."

"Even if I were to find a woman I loved," he said slowly, "I wouldn't marry. I've been on my own all of my life. In schools, in the army, then living a bachelor's life. It would be too much of an adjustment. That aside—" he added quickly, seeing that she was about to say something "—I think I'd always fear she'd leave me eventually."

It made more sense than his blind loyalty to Jacob.

"Not all women leave."

"Fears aren't always logical," he mused.

"I know." There seemed little more to say. She stood up. "Let's walk. Maybe we'll come up with a way to stop driving each other crazy."

They left the car behind and strolled through the streets of the ancient lower town of Elbia. Thomas told her of its beginnings, back in the eleventh century as part of the Holy Roman Empire. He pointed out crumbling foundations, the place where a grand Herrenhouse once had stood, and a fountain built to honor Jacob's great-grandfather Wilhelm. The city had a glorious past, and she loved feeling part of it. It had the elegance she'd seen in postcards of Vienna, the charm of Paris and a history to compete with the grandest cities of the world but on a smaller scale.

At last she stopped, and when Thomas faced her she took his large hands in her smaller ones and looked up at him. "Enough of the past, time for the present."

"I was afraid of that." He smiled weakly and rolled his eyes.

"I don't want to leave Elbia just yet," she said. "I love it here, and I think you were right— I do need a break...and time to figure out what I want to do with my life."

"Then stay."

"I've never met a man like you, Thomas," she said truthfully. "I can't pretend I don't feel things when we're together that I never felt with other men. And I'm very, very happy you are tempted to sleep with me. That makes me feel special."

"I'm glad." He gazed down at her warily.

"But I respect your reasons for not wanting to become seriously involved. And although I told you Jacob's opinion and your concerns for my future shouldn't matter, I think that's wrong. They do matter a lot. I shouldn't ask you to be disloyal to Jacob. And I shouldn't embark on an affair when getting emotionally involved with a man should be the last thing on my mind right now."

"I agree," he said cautiously. Two words seemed to be his limit. She thought very hard about her own next words. "Perhaps we should also agree to keep our relationship uncomplicated. I value your friendship. Can we keep it at that?"

"I've tried," he pointed out.

"But I wasn't helping, was I?"

He shook his head, his eyes darkening at remembered moments.

"This time I will help," she promised. "I won't tease you or try to tempt you into compromising your honor. And if you should feel yourself weakening, tell me, and I'll make myself scarce for a few days…take a trip to Austria or Switzerland or somewhere. That's not exactly a hardship."

He smiled. "No, it isn't." Lifting her fingertips to his lips he kissed them lightly. "You can trust me to abide by our pledge."

"Friends," she whispered, her eyes tickling with tears she refused to shed.

"Friends," he repeated, as he released her hand and drew a long, deep breath.

Diane followed his gaze to the castle rising majestically above them. She felt warm and good and right inside. She'd never known a man she liked as much as Thomas, and after their conversation she respected him, too. Someday, if she was very lucky, she would find someone at least half as fine as he, and if that man had room in his heart for one decent woman with three children…she would be his forever.

Five

Thomas had given his promise, and he did his best to keep it. But no matter how hard he tried to think of Diane as no more than a friend and member of the royal family during the following weeks, he always returned to the memory of her eyes softly glazing over as he leaned down to trap her urgent gasps of pleasure within their impassioned kisses. Neither could he forget the way she'd urgently seized his wrist and pressed his hand harder against her, so desperately eager for the release she hadn't experienced in months, years, or perhaps ever.

He had come perilously close to losing himself in sympathy with her rapture.

The power she held over him was amazing, even frightening. He'd fed off her pleasure, been content to give her all she wanted and needed that day in the stable. That was something else that had never happened with other women. He had made sure they were satisfied, yes, but for selfish reasons—to make certain if he wanted a return engagement they would be eager. With Diane, he thought only of her and what would make her happy.

Later he'd had to deal with the painful consequence of his own urgent need. He'd wished her delicate fingers had been holding him. Instead he had to settle for a very cold shower.

Now, standing before the long, crowded shelves of the palace library, Thomas thrust aside these unwanted visions before his body reacted again. Just in time, because he suddenly became aware of footsteps entering the room. When he looked up from the heavy legal tome Jacob had sent him to find, he saw a smiling Diane, glowing in a yellow sundress.

He was lost.

"You've been avoiding me," she accused him lightly.

"I've been busy. I do work here, you remember."

"I know. Just teasing. I don't expect you to entertain me."

"New dress?" he commented. The bodice was cut straight across the front with wide gingham straps over her shoulders. Modest swells of her breasts were visible above the smooth cotton band and sent a quick electric charge through him.

"Yes, it is new." She looked pleased that he'd noticed and spun girlishly to model it for him. "Allison took me shopping yesterday. She says the color complements my dark hair."

"It does," he agreed, then settled into silence because he didn't dare remark on all the other ways she looked beautiful that morning.

"I was thinking," she said slowly. "It would be a lovely day for a picnic in the valley. Do you know of a nice spot?"

"Yes, several," he said cautiously. "Who is going?"

"Allison and the children and I. Jacob, if he can get away…and you're invited."

He heaved an inward sigh of relief. As long as he wasn't alone with her, it would make for an enjoyable day. "That sounds very pleasant indeed."

She smiled. "Good. You decide where we should go. I'll go see what Cook can pack for our feast."

She left him in such a muddle of emotions it was hopeless. His heart raced then felt light within his chest, like a fledgling bird taking wing for the first time. It would be wonderful to lounge in the sunshine with the five people who had become most important to his world. Moreover, it would be safe, and he was grateful for that.

But another part of him yearned to throw off caution and find a way to have Diane to himself for just a few hours. He wouldn't touch her, he vowed. He'd just listen to her laughter, soak up the music of her voice, store away the sparkle in her eyes. They would talk as they had in the village, about their pasts, their hopes for the future…the simple, everyday things all friends talk about. He had some ideas he wanted to share with her about how she might use her college degree to support herself and the children more comfortably than by baby-sitting. He knew a CEO of a large New York-based company who owed him a favor.

He sensed she would never again suggest they become lovers. She was a strong woman. She had made up her mind to file him in a category that didn't allow physical intimacy, because he had said that was the only way they could be friends. But he could still see Diane's sweet expression, her eyes fluttering closed as he pleasured her.

Life was so unfair.

Assuming Jacob would want him to act as chauffeur for their trip down into the lush valley below the castle, Thomas fueled the limo, then took his time polishing its sleek, black finish before pulling round from the garages to the kitchen entrance. He only had to wait twenty more minutes before Diane appeared with a large wicker basket slung over her arm.

"Where are the others?" he asked.

"On their way down, I guess," she said smiling. "I left blankets to lay on the ground in the kitchen. Could you go get them?"

Thomas ducked below the stone arch into the cool, dim main kitchen at the back of the house. It was used only for large parties and required a staff of at least eight to run efficiently. The smaller family kitchen was behind that, and he heard the intercom buzz then a voice crackle over it. He walked in to find Cook listening intently to Allison's voice.

"...so please tell my sister that I don't dare take Cray out today. We'll take a rain check on the picnic."

Thomas scowled. "What's this about?"

Cook jumped and spun away from the intercom on the wall to face him. *"Mein Gott!"*

"Entschuldigung," he apologized. "I didn't meant to startle you, Frau Seubel. I take it there's been a change in plans?"

"The little prince isn't well," she explained in German. "An upset tummy, says the queen."

"And Jacob and the baby?"

She observed him as if he were mad. "You expect the king to go on a picnic without his wife?"

"You're right. How silly of me." He observed the toes of his shoes. "Then I guess it's off."

Cook sighed. "All that lovely food. Why don't you and Frau Fields go on your own?" she suggested.

Thomas stared at her. Why don't we go on our own?

After the obvious answer crossed his mind as a vivid playback of the last time they'd been together, he settled his shoulders and chewed his bottom lip in concentration. Why not indeed? Two mature adults should be capable of sharing a simple meal together. One way or another, he would feel obliged to keep Diane company in lieu of the family excursion.

He turned on his heel and burst into the sunshine to find Diane comfortably ensconced in the third seat of the limo, leaving plenty of room for the four absent members of their party. Leaning through the open window, he gave her a lopsided smile. "Looks like we're faced with a dilemma."

"What's that?"

"Cray is under the weather. Nothing serious, but that means he and Allison won't be coming. And Jacob won't take time out from his work without her to coax him."

"So, it's just us?" She looked away from him and across the garden.

"We can either cancel, too, or go ahead as planned."

She studied the azure sky and pouted. "I was so

looking forward to the afternoon. But I suppose another day..."

"Not necessarily," Thomas said, and her head snapped around.

"You've got to be kidding."

"Why shouldn't the two of us go ahead with our picnic? We're friends, aren't we?"

"Friends who have admitted there's a load of steam bubbling under the surface," she reminded him.

"Steam can be controlled."

She was shaking her head, her hazel eyes sparking with green, skeptical. "Maybe in a public place, but out there in—"

"I have faith in both of us," he assured her. "Listen, I know you want to go. It's been nearly two weeks since we made our pact, and we've stuck to it."

"Fine," she said after a small hesitation. "But I'm moving up to the front seat with you. I feel ridiculous riding alone in the back of this monstrosity."

They drove through some of the most spectacular scenery Diane had ever seen. The grass in the valley was so lush and green she doubted it ever browned out in the summer. A river splashed through the center of the valley, branching into tiny rivulets, providing a natural irrigation system. Edelweiss, lingonberry bushes and sweet lavender grew in abundance. They drove down one side of the mountain, through the town, then up a rise on the other side of the dell. Thomas pulled the car off the road at a spot overlooking the entire valley with the castle's turrets shining in the distance.

"It doesn't look real," Diane said. "It's like an illustration out of a book of fairy tales."

"Not too many castles in Connecticut, hmm?"

She smiled. "Only a few." Flinging open her door she jumped out.

Thomas watched her for a moment, content for the time being to simply be near her.

"Well, come on!" she shouted. "I'm starving. Let's unload this food."

Together they pulled tightly wrapped paper packets of German sausages, pungent cheeses, two kinds of breads and a seven-layer cake with mocha cream, which Thomas told her was called Doboschtorte. They arranged their feast around them on the blanket. Diane broke off a chunk of crusty bread for herself and one for Thomas. They ate in silence, and he turned his face up into the sunshine and thought he had never been happier.

"This is wonderful," she said at last, dusting crumbs from her lap as she licked the last traces of rich whipped cream from her fingertips. "I can't remember feeling this relaxed in years."

"You've had the sole responsibility for three children and running a household," Thomas commented. "I expect you didn't get many days off."

"No," she admitted with a careless shrug. "I guess I didn't. But I've never resented time spent with or for my children."

He studied her strong profile, softened by the summer sun. She was far more appealing to him, without makeup and in yellow gingham, than any spa-buffed contessa decked out in jewels.

"It's nice, though, just for a change...not having to prepare every meal, do two loads of laundry every day, scrub crayon off the wall or sop up spilled orange juice."

"I would imagine." He chuckled.

She lay back on the blanket, and her dark hair spread beneath her head and neck, framing her sun-blushed face. "Thomas, have you ever thought about being a father?"

The question took him by surprise. "No. Well, yes, but not for long." He laughed nervously.

"Why? I've seen you with Cray and Christina. You're so gentle and sweet with them. I think you'd make a wonderful father."

How had they gotten onto this bloody subject? He leaned on one elbow and looked past Diane to the mountains, chill and distant, emotionless. At least mountains never changed. You knew what to expect of them. They simply existed, solid, dependable, year after year. People were different. People led you to believe they would be there forever, to protect and love you. Then one day they were gone...or they pushed you out of their life.

"Don't, Diane," he whispered hoarsely.

She turned on her side to face him, her eyes shining, urgent with questions and concerns he didn't want to hear. "Have you ever tried to find your mother? To ask her why she left?"

He glared at her, demanding without words that she stop. She was treading on forbidden ground. One look at his stormy expression and she should have known that.

"Thomas, please. I'm not trying to pry. It may be she felt she had no choice. Maybe she regrets what she did and would have come back for you if she hadn't felt so ashamed."

"Stop!" he growled.

Shocked, she blinked at him, opened her mouth tentatively, then closed her lips in a firm line.

"The past doesn't matter. It's over. Done!" he snapped, sitting up stiffly.

Diane looked up at his anguished profile. He was such a strong man, physically, and he put up an impressively fierce and dispassionate front. Anyone who didn't know him would believe he was immune to tender emotions. But she saw through the veneer he'd so carefully applied, layer by layer over the years, to protect himself from love that could destroy when it was taken away. Inside he was as vulnerable as she, perhaps more so.

Diane wished she could offer him some comfort, some small hope and understanding that love didn't have to be a prelude to rejection and heartache. Why she knew these things, she couldn't have said. Her own marriage certainly hadn't been a good example of a loving relationship. But she believed in her heart that for every person who yearned to love, there was a perfect partner who offered love in return, someone who completed that person. With luck, two people fated to be together would find each other. There were no guarantees, of course. But she believed in possibilities.

"Thomas," she breathed, laying her hand on his arm.

He tensed under her gently curled fingers. His eyes went suddenly flat, dull. "Don't." Diane could feel him withdrawing from her. She could sense his pain and wanted to heal him. His isolation tore at her heart.

"You said yourself, the past is over. What you

choose for yourself is up to you. Your parents' mistakes can't determine your future.''

''You don't know what you're talking about,'' he muttered darkly.

She leaned toward him, her lips inches from his ear. ''Then explain it to me. Tell me why you—''

He was up off the blanket and striding away from her across the meadow before the last word faded from her lips. His entire body was rigid with fury. His broad shoulders hunched, his fists swinging at his sides, his neck muscles bulged and she could feel the power that wanted to lash out, barely checked in his large frame.

What had she done?

Quickly she leaped to her feet and raced after him, the tall grass lashing at her bare legs. The ground was uneven. Her feet were bare and hit hidden furrows, and her ankle twisted. Down she went with a strangled gasp in a graceless tangle.

Her first thought was for her injured foot, but she immediately realized nothing serious had happened in the fall. Feeling foolish, she was about to pull herself up off the ground when something blocked the sun. She looked up at the source of the shadow, at Thomas. His hand reached down toward her. His expression was no longer dangerous, at least not in an angry way.

''Come,'' he said, gripping her wrist to pull her to her feet.

She opened her mouth to speak. He shook his head and brought her fingers to his lips. It was the tenderest of gestures she could imagine from such a bear of a man.

"I suppose we've both known pain," she murmured. "Different kinds."

He looked down at her with an intensity that sent shivers through her, and she wished she could read his thoughts. He neither denied nor affirmed her statement, but she knew somehow in her heart that she was right. He was tormented, and he wouldn't admit why...perhaps not even to himself. She felt sure it was something more than his own parents' inability to give him the love he'd needed as a child.

"Do you think two people in pain might find a way to heal one another?" she whispered.

"Without causing more damage?" His voice was a tight rasp.

She smiled. "That would be the goal." Her fingers reached up around his neck to flick through the shorter hairs at his nape. She could feel him leaning toward her almost imperceptibly. "Thomas."

"Yes?"

"Kiss me. Please."

He closed his eyes, and the muscles in his face worked, strained, locked.

"Kiss me," she whispered again.

"Can't."

"Why not?"

"If I do—" he opened his eyes and looked down at her again, and she knew she'd never seen real passion in a man's eyes until that moment "—if I do, I will have to make love to you, Diane. I will have no choice."

"Then make love to me. Here. Now."

She sensed as she said the words that she'd turned her life in a new and unalterable direction. She had stepped out of the shelter of her old and predictable existence into a world beyond the rules. A tidy Cape Cod on a tree-lined street, household tasks, children with scraped knees and hungry tummies, bills to be paid—all faded away, to be replaced by her own needs, so long ignored.

With a soaring heart she stood, weak-kneed as Thomas bent to kiss her. His warm lips settled over hers. His arms wrapped around her and closed protectively about her shoulders, sealing out the real world, promising bliss as he pressed her cheek to his chest.

No one had passed through or within sight of the meadow while they'd eaten, and as they walked back to their blanket holding hands, she trusted that Thomas knew no one would disturb them. He kissed her deeply, savoring her as if to later remember this time. He brought her down among the blades of tall grass, and they were screened by nature from even the distant world.

For a fleeting moment she wondered if the way he was touching her now was the way he had touched all women before her. But something told her this was not so. His hands trembled against her flesh as if he was breaking new ground, as if the experience was as virgin to him as it was to her.

Diane looked up at Thomas, framed both sides of his wide face with her cool palms. She wanted to tell him how thankful she was for this moment but was terrified a single word from her lips would break the spell. He fumbled with the buttons down the front of her sundress, and she waited, patiently breathing in the male scent of him, kissing him softly across his forehead, his chin, the corners of his lips, believing in nothing but these precious minutes.

Because the sundress had its own bra, she wore nothing but cotton panties beneath it. As the bodice separated down the front, her breasts spilled out and warmed in the sun. Thomas's hands caressed them, lavishing equal attention on each, then he drew back and solemnly observed the effect. She didn't have to look to know her nipples were dark saucers, peaked hard from his touch. She tingled, burned, hungered for more.

Diane arched her back, thrusting herself toward him in invitation. She ached to feel his mouth close over her tingling breasts. How often had she fantasized about him kissing her there and so many other forbidden places? As if he knew, he lowered his head and brushed his lips across her raised nipples. Cupping her breasts in his two strong hands, he brought his mouth down over one, drew her between his sharp, white teeth, slid his tongue in fiery circles until she shuddered and whimpered in delight.

His kisses nestled between her breasts, and she clutched him to her. He worked his way down over the velvet plane of her stomach to her navel. There he paused to tease with his tongue and glance up at her, questioningly. His eyes were as black as the darkest night; she could feel his heart pounding against her thighs through the heaving wall of his chest.

"I want all of you," he whispered hoarsely.

"And I need you," she told him urgently.

He nodded even as his hands moved slowly to her hips and drew her panties down her long legs and gently placed them on the grass. He easily parted her legs but slid down her outstretched body rather than up. She gasped in surprise as he lowered his head and repeated his plunging kisses of her lips, this time relishing far more intimate feminine terrain. Diane cried out in shocked approval, threading her fingers through his hair, rejoicing in the flames that licked her from deep within. He stroked her with his tongue and the firm pads of his thumbs until she thought she'd go mad with the pleasure of it.

Diane let herself go, completely.

The world was no more than a swirl of colors. Trees, grass, clouds all spun around her as waves of sensation washed over and through her, lifting her so high she no longer felt the earth beneath her. She was one with the sky, with eternity, with life itself.

At last she lay limp in the sweet grass, her body humming, her thighs honeyed with her own ecstasy, her head dizzy with release. Surely no other woman ever felt this deliciously spent. And no other man knew how to make his lover feel this—

"Not yet, darling," Thomas whispered as she squinted up into the sun at him.

"Wha—?"

"We're just getting started."

"We're what?" Her glance dropped lower. "Oh—my goodness!" Although he still wore his shirt, he had unzipped and slid down his jeans along with anything he might have worn underneath. He was in perfect proportion with the rest of his proud, six-foot, five-inch body. Shyly, she reached out to touch him. He was full and firm and beautiful. And hers.

Of all her fantasies, her most cherished was to be loved wildly and freely by such a man as this. Even if it never happened again, she'd know for the rest of her life that she had once belonged to Thomas just as he belonged to her. Now, as she gazed on the physical evidence of his eagerness for her, she chuckled, and their eyes met as she communicated to him that she was in no way laughing at him. She was laughing because it felt just plain marvelous to laugh and anticipate sharing her body with him again, in another wonderful way.

She opened herself to him. He moved between her thighs, gauging her expression, a fierce possessiveness rising in his eyes as he found her and plunged his full length within her in one sharp thrust that sent her reeling and clutching at his shoulders. She was glad, so very glad that he wasn't being overly gentle, because she wanted the savage in him, wanted him unrestricted by manners, the past, and all that had held him away from her since the day they'd met.

Everything Thomas had sternly told himself he must not do, he did.

He understood, even as he buried himself fiercely within her, that he was sabotaging the plan he'd formed as he'd driven Diane to their picnic site. He saw each error as he made it, and he cursed himself for being weak. But he simply hadn't been able to stop himself. He'd told himself he wouldn't lay a hand on the woman…but he'd so wanted to taste her lips, and he had. That had been what had set him off, because in taking her up on her invitation for a kiss, he then needed to taste her everywhere. And once he'd witnessed her delicious reaction to his making love to her with his hands and mouth, he was hopelessly the victim of his own hunger.

It was as if, now that he'd given her pleasure, he could deny himself nothing. And she was so very welcoming, so very eager to please.

Only after he'd entered her did a distant corner of

his mind register a warning. Never would he have chanced relations with another woman without protection, but this day had come as a complete surprise to him and he hadn't been prepared. As he felt himself slide neatly, slickly, delectably inside her—flesh against flesh—he cursed himself for not caring about anything but this moment. Besides, he was safe for her: he had always been careful before this and he would reassure her when it was over. As for Diane, he knew she didn't sleep around, and her husband had been gone from her bed for nearly a year. If she'd been aware of a reason why they shouldn't be intimate, she would have told him.

What worried him was the other issue. Neither of them could afford an unwanted pregnancy.

As Thomas knit his wide fingers through her slender ones and pressed her hands into the soft blanket, he moved himself deeper and faster. He sensed that only seconds remained. Concentrating until the last possible moment, he at last pulled himself free with a reluctant groan.

He caught only a glimpse of puckish smile on her lips before he collapsed beside her, his muscled leg draped over her hips, his arms wrapped round her head, crushing her to him as he hit the wall between the ultimate male bliss and the shock of reality.

He had committed treason…and he didn't care. All that mattered was that Diane was his. For these precious seconds she was part of him, all he'd ever wanted and more than he deserved. Until forced to release her, he wouldn't let go.

Six

Thomas felt Diane shift beneath him. He gently lifted his leg to give her room. "Are you all right?"

"I'm fine." She beamed up at him. "That was—" she shook her head "—beyond words."

She did look sublimely happy. He was certainly glad of that. But now came the hard part, and he didn't know how to broach the subject in any way but bluntly.

"I'm sorry. I should have used a condom."

"I suppose," she murmured, touching her palm to his shirtfront. "You know, some day, I'd really like to see all of you naked at the same time."

"I'm serious, Diane. It was irresponsible of me not to. We hadn't discussed our histories. I want to reassure you, I've never done that before…gone without protection."

"I wasn't worried," she said, sitting up to watch

him tuck in his shirt, pleating it at the sides, military-style.

"You *should* worry about such things, now that you're single again."

She shrugged as if to say she understood, but right now she didn't want to discuss anything so unromantic. "Anyway, thank you for taking the only precaution you could. It's been so long, it never occurred to me to even think about the possibility of pregnancy." She blushed prettily, looking suddenly embarrassed.

He watched as she finished tidying herself up, and felt himself react again as she dressed. Amazingly, he wanted her again.

This time, he resisted. "Come, let's eat. You were hungry before. You must be famished by now."

As they shared the meal Cook had prepared for six instead of two, Thomas watched Diane for any signs of regret for what they'd just done. But she glowed brighter than the sunshine. She laughed and told him stories of her younger years. She had nearly joined the Peace Corps in her senior year of college, but then she'd found out she was pregnant with her first child. And her life had abruptly changed course.

"You never thought of giving up the baby?" he asked.

"No," she said without hesitation.

"You wouldn't have felt compelled to marry Gary then," he pointed out.

"I realize that, and I won't say that the thought never crossed my mind." She bit into a crisp apple. "But I knew I could never give up a baby. And when I told Gary, he was the one who suggested we marry. He said he wanted to share the responsibility of raising our child."

"And did he?"

"For a while." Diane took another bite of her fruit thoughtfully, then chewed faster. "Let's talk about other things."

The afternoon wore on, and they spent it eating, chatting and holding hands beneath a brilliant sun. Thomas felt like a teenage boy again, discovering girls were different. Only this time he was detecting a finer line—that one woman was different from so many others. He couldn't get enough of Diane's laughter and smiles. In all the times he'd seen her, she'd never seemed this happy. Although he was pleased, her carefree attitude troubled him more and more as the sun dropped lower in the sky. Now that they'd crossed a line that was never meant to be crossed, what would happen?

"We should be getting back," he murmured, leaning over to kiss her lightly on the lips as she lay gazing up at the clouds overhead.

"I know." She frowned prettily at him. "I don't want this day to end."

"Neither do I." And he meant it.

"I take it you still think Jacob wouldn't be pleased to hear that we—"

"He would be livid."

Diane studied him, lifted a finger to trace the contours of his face. She looked more curious than upset. "The king's right-hand man isn't allowed a personal life?"

"Of course I am, but that's separate from my duties to the royal family and the court."

"I see," she breathed out each word distinctly, "all...very...discreet."

"Yes."

Her eyes were twinkling too mischievously for his comfort. "And we've been discreet. Why can't we continue?"

He had to make her understand this wasn't a game. "What happened between us here, today…it can't happen again, Diane."

"Why not?" she asked simply.

He was astounded. "We didn't plan this. It just happened. And it was—"

"Wonderful," she filled in for him, smiling from ear to ear.

"Yes," he agreed. "It was. But we can't carry on an affair under the king's roof and—"

"Dear me, no! I'm sure the royal palace of Elbia has never been witness to an affair. No duke every chased a lady-in-waiting up a turret. No queen ever had it on with the stable boy. How shocking!"

He shook a finger at her. "You're making fun of me. I'm serious."

She narrowed her eyes at him. "Why do you think I'm not serious, too?"

"Don't make this any harder than it already is for me. I'm trying to do the right thing for Jacob's sake, but also for yours."

Her smile was suddenly gone. Rich gray-green eyes changed to cold granite. "For *my* sake? You're *protecting* me, is that what you're saying?"

"Yes," he said. sighing, relieved that she finally understood.

"From what?" she demanded loudly.

Or maybe she didn't. "From disappointment. You know there is no future for us."

"I told you before, it doesn't matter to me. It's enough to feel alive again! To feel special, to lose control, to respond to a man the way you make me…respond." She flashed her eyes at him. "I discovered something today, Thomas. I enjoy being touched. I enjoy forgetting where I am, what time of day it is, and…and even who I am! And I—"

"Enough," he said firmly. How could he possibly do the honorable thing when she talked like this? The more she argued with him the more he wanted to throw her down in a patch of wildflowers and start all over again. And he wasn't going to do that! "You have a home across the ocean, a life to return to."

"At the end of the summer. Yes, all of that is waiting for me, and I'll return to Nanticoke to pick up where I left off. But while I'm here, I mean to do exactly what you said I should do while I'm on vacation."

He glared at her. "Dare I ask that you remind me?"

"Relax and *enjoy* myself. And I can't think of anything I've enjoyed more in all of my life than making love with you."

She was so forthright about her feelings, it took him aback. He was accustomed to circumspect women. Women who hid their emotions and buried their hearts under bank accounts and hidden social agendas. He didn't know what to say. Then he felt her hand on his arm, and he looked down to meet her questioning eyes.

"Maybe I misunderstood the way you were with me," she said softly. "I felt it was so very special, and I assumed it was that special for you, too. But I'll understand if you tell me that this one time was enough for you."

"What is enough and what must be are two dif-

ferent things," he said stiffly. "I didn't have the right
to do what I did in the first place. I can't compound
the sin by repeating it." He started tossing food back
into the picnic baskets. "Let's get back to the castle
before your sister becomes suspicious."

Diane met his eyes and held them for several seconds, then nodded slowly.

Thomas didn't know what more he could say to
her. He felt utterly helpless. To lead Diane on would
be cruel. They had so little in common that a long-
term relationship would be impossible. Beyond concerns for just the two of them, her children needed a
father—someone they could depend upon. He wasn't
that man and never could be. So he had no choice but
to leave the door open for a man better than he—a
man who would stand by her.

Diane spent the following days exploring anew the
castle's many chambers, storage rooms, hidden passages and collections of art and historic treasures.
Sometimes she was in the company of Allison, and
they became young girls again, giggling at imagined
ghosts, knights and legends of an ancient world. Other
times Diane preferred to be on her own, to wander
the stone halls hung with rich tapestries or stand on
a balcony overlooking the courtyard, the town beyond
and the wildflower-strewn meadows leading up to the
mountains. She remembered vividly the touch of
Thomas's sometimes gentle, sometimes demanding
hands on her body. If she closed her eyes and
breathed quietly, she could almost feel him still
within her.

She felt guilty for wanting him so. He was staying
away from her for reasons she didn't fully compre-

hend, but they were reasons he believed were honorable. How could she blame him for placing honor above passion? If she'd thought she was capable of seducing the man, she probably would have tried. Then she would feel badly for making him break his vow. She had told him, on their way back to the castle that day, that once was enough to last her a lifetime, if that was how it must be.

She'd lied. Every waking hour, she yearned for him.

Despite grieving for her lost lover, time did pass. Another week was soon gone, and Allison commandeered Diane to help with plans for the lavish summer festivities marking the anniversary of the von Auster- and family's coming to power in Elbia nearly five hundred years before.

It was on the afternoon of a reception for visiting foreign dignitaries that Diane took a wrong turn and ended up in an unfamiliar wing. She turned around and headed back toward the central part of the castle when she caught a whiff of a bold scent that sent ripples of lovely sensation through her. She stopped before a door not entirely closed.

Slowly she moved toward it, and the scent grew stronger. The connection struck her all at once. Thomas.

This was Thomas's aftershave—a blend of musk, smoky sweetness and leather. She breathed in the intoxicating essence, and her limbs felt rubbery. Flashes of him backed by green meadow rushed through her mind. She envisioned his tautly ridged stomach, poised over her, revealed by his opened shirt. The muscles contracted with the rhythm of their union, moving in synchrony with their dance of love. She closed her eyes and shuddered.

A voice urgently called out his name, and she was shocked to realize it was her own. "Thomas?" she repeated more softly, hoping he was in his chambers, for this must be the apartment he'd spoken of. His territory. His private sanctuary from the royal family when he was off duty.

"Thomas?" she called again, then knocked on the heavy wooden doorjamb. "Are you decent?"

Music was playing inside. American jazz. A saxophone crooning low and sensual tones against a ripple of piano notes. She hadn't realized Thomas liked jazz, and this set her musing as to how little she really did know about him. He was a private man, except for the stoic face he chose to reveal to others. She wondered what other tastes he enjoyed that she didn't know about. She wanted to sit and talk with him as they had that distant day in the town. What kinds of foods did he love? Did he like opera better than jazz? Did he prefer Shakespeare to Neil Simon? Van Gogh over Rembrandt? Did he sleep in pajamas—top and bottom—or in the nude?

She giggled. Well, that last was definitely a bit prurient. Perhaps she wouldn't ask that.

"Thomas?" She gently pushed the door open wide enough to step through.

His chambers were very much like hers—a single expansive room, the stone walls hidden behind modern plaster—but for the one side where the fireplace took up the twelve-foot expanse from floor to ceiling. Modern plumbing had been added at some time, necessitating a portion of the area to be partitioned off as a bathroom. There was a dressing area at one side, at the other a niche surrounded by three windows that sheltered a massive, dark wooden desk with dozens of little drawers for storing things. The bed itself was an enormous four-poster that looked purely British. It rose high off the stone floor, surrounded by opulent Oriental carpets.

It was obvious Thomas wasn't in residence at the moment. She should leave, she told herself.

But she couldn't. Too much of him was here. It would be like walking out of his life, and although she knew that would be inevitable at the end of the summer, it came too soon now.

Diane crossed the room slowly, moving toward his bed. The intimacy of the cluster of personal belongings on the square mahogany table near the head touched her deeply. A pair of reading glasses she hadn't known he wore. A half-filled ceramic mug of water. A bottle of aspirin. A leather-bound volume of Goethe, in German, the ancient script unfathomable to her. She stroked the softly grained cover with her fingertips and imagined she felt Thomas's hand over hers.

Three gold-framed photographs stood beside a brass lamp. One was of the royal family—Jacob, Allison, the two children. It was a formal portrait, but Diane noted a sparkle in her sister's eyes that was genuine. Jacob stood behind her and to one side, but gave an impression of surrounding her and their babies protectively. She smiled. Theirs was a fairy tale that had ended happily.

The other two photos were much older. Thirty or more years, she would guess, from the subjects' clothing and faded colors of the prints. One was of a man of fair complexion and aristocratic bearing. He was staring directly into the camera with a stern expression. Although he didn't much resemble Thomas, she was certain this was his father. He looked like a man without heart. A man who wouldn't blink at sending his child off to live with strangers. It was the way of the British upper crust; she understood that. But she imagined some parents still might find the tradition a sad one. This man wouldn't miss a little boy.

The other photograph was of a woman. A beautiful, dark-haired, dark-eyed woman. She had a long aquiline nose, a proud tilt to her head, high cheekbones and elegant, though broad, shoulders. The resemblance was amazing. If a sketch artist had been asked to draw a feminine version of Thomas, this would be she. Stood side by side, Thomas and his mother would never be mistaken for other than mother and son.

She reached down and picked up the picture in its gilt frame and held it, studying the woman's face. What sort of mother walked away from three sons and a husband and never came back? Had she been swept away by a secret lover? Had she run in fear from an abusive aristocratic husband, then kept forcibly away from her children by his solicitors?

"What are you doing?" a voice roared from behind her.

Diane gasped and spun around, the photograph still gripped in her trembling hands. Thomas stood in the open doorway, glowering at her.

"I was just—"

"Give that to me!" He was across the wide room in four quick strides that seemed to take no time at all.

She opened her fingers as he wrenched the photograph from them. "I'm sorry, I didn't mean to—"

"Out!" he boomed. "Get out of my room. You have no right to touch my things."

Diane was shaking so hard she knew she couldn't take a step without her knees buckling beneath her. But his accusation stung. She couldn't leave without setting him straight.

"I didn't intend to disturb you or your belongings. I was lost and came on your apartment by accident." She was gasping for breath as if she'd run a mile.

He loomed over her, rage contorting his once-handsome face. "And I suppose you accidentally found yourself clear across the room, rifling through my personal possessions?"

"No, I—"

He lurched forward a step. She fell back three smaller ones, curving around him toward the door. As she glanced down at the photograph in his hand, a surprising thought struck her. The physical resemblance between mother and son was obvious. But did Thomas see the comparison stopping there? Or did he believe—

"Thomas, no one inherits a gene for desertion."

He straightened another two inches and glared down at her. His expression was threatening, but also tormented. "Get out!" he growled.

"It's true, isn't it? You think because *she* left you and your brothers, you won't be able to stand by a family."

He said nothing, but his eyes transformed from earthy-brown to obsidian—sharp chips of volcanic stone that might reverse their chemical nature and glow with dangerous life again.

"There's a big difference between what two people look like and their souls." Tears of sympathy gathered in her eyes. "You and your mother are two individual—"

"Leave me alone!" he roared, lunging forward in anger.

She skittered backward, bumped into the wall beside the doorway, then slid quickly through it. The heavy iron-studded door slammed in her face, but not before she caught a last blurry image of Thomas through her tears, his thick brows low over black, black eyes...pulse throbbing in his temple...fists clenching and unclenching as if he would have most certainly struck her had she been a man.

She stood in the hallway, shaking, trying to catch her breath, shocked by the fury she'd witnessed. She'd seen Thomas react explosively when a pack of reporters descended on Jacob and Allison just after they'd been married. And again, at the airport in New York, when a crowd of curious onlookers threatened to crush Allison and her children in their enthusiasm to greet her. His protective instincts had sometimes turned to rage. But he had never faced her down like this, as if *she* were the enemy.

Diane gulped down two more breaths, turned on her heel and dashed down the long hallway. If she still couldn't find her way back to the central part of the castle, she would wait until one of the staff happened by. No way would she go back to Thomas for directions!

Thomas collapsed on the edge of his bed, tossed the gold-framed photo in the vague direction of the pillows and dropped his head into his hands. For days he had fought the desperate urge to see Diane again. He had made himself scarce from the family's private rooms where he might run into her. He had risen early for work and stayed at his tasks late. When forced to join the royal family at a meal, he'd handled it by involving Jacob and Allison in complex business conversations Diane would be unlikely to participate in.

But when he found her standing beside his bed, where no other woman had ever been allowed, studying his most private possessions—he'd totally lost it.

What right did she have to intrude on his life and analyze him? If he'd been able to be a different sort of man, he would have been! Since he couldn't, he'd learned to accept being alone, except for an occasional brief affair with a beautiful woman. This was as close to happiness as he deserved or dared reach for.

But Diane had torn away the barriers of cold logic he'd so carefully constructed. She stood brazenly beside his bed and told him he wasn't his mother. For a brief moment a flicker of hope had lightened his heart before fading away to leave him once more in torment.

Diane knew that the night of the grand ball marking the height of Elbia's festivities would be the most difficult of her life. Even though the castle's ballroom would be packed with guests, orchestra, serving staff and select members of the press…Thomas would also be there. It broke her heart that this might be the last time she'd see him, for she'd decided to cut her vacation short and return to Nanticoke as soon as Jacob's plane was available. That might be as early as the next morning.

That night she dressed carefully in the champagne satin gown Allison had helped her choose from among those designed by a seamstress in town. Diane couldn't imagine a more beautiful dress. The fabric gleamed softly. Panels formed elegant gores from the hips to the hem, widening to a graceful flair, lending the skirt a fluid motion when she walked. The off-the-shoulder style settled perfectly over the curve of her upper arms. The dress was sleeveless, and the seamstress suggested long, fitted gloves of the same fabric to mold her slim arms from fingertips to elbows.

"After the formal reception line, you can take them off," Allison told her, then added in a whisper, "It's much easier to dance without gloves. They make my hands sweat."

Diane didn't suppose she'd do much dancing that night, but when the time came she was surprised to find how many gentlemen were eager to whisk her in a romantic waltz or swirling polka across the polished parquet floor. Yet no matter how many times she whirled beneath the blazing crystal chandeliers on the arm of one distinguished partner or another, she was still acutely aware of Thomas's presence in the ballroom. He seemed rarely without a lovely, admiring female in his arms. And those who didn't get a chance to dance with the dark-haired man who stood two heads taller than most everyone else in the room flirted shamelessly with him.

Diane wished she could feel justified in the irritation she felt whenever a pair of sparkling blue eyes nailed him. But, she sadly thought, she had no more claim to him than any other woman in the room.

At last the pain of watching him and knowing that

after she left he'd have no trouble finding another companion for picnics in the meadow became too much for her. She told Allison she had a bad headache and took herself off to her room to be alone. She had packing to do. As soon as she finished tossing clothing into suitcases, she would turn out the light and try to sleep. Although only a little after ten o'clock, she felt as if she hadn't slept in an eternity.

Even from her room in the east wing, she could hear the elegant strains of the violins, the sweeping rhythms of the Viennese waltzes…and she could still see in her mind's eye Thomas in his dashing tuxedo, his wide shoulders rising above the rest of the guests as he held a woman in his arms who should have been her.

She felt infinite sadness. Deep loss. But there is no fighting destiny, Diane told herself.

She sadly unzipped the satin gown and stepped out of it. It drifted to the floor with a soft whoosh. She left it there while she washed up and pulled a cotton nightshirt over her head. When she came out of the bathroom, Thomas was standing in the middle of the room, the gown in his large hands.

Diane swallowed and wrapped her arms around her ribs, as if to shield herself from his piercing gaze, even though she was already modestly covered. She couldn't speak. The fire in his eyes left her speechless.

"Why are you leaving?"

"I had a headache. I told Allison I—"

"Not the ball…Elbia!" he snapped at her. "Allison said she thought you were planning to return home soon. And here are packed bags. Why?"

"There are things to be done," she said simply.

"It's because of us, isn't it?"

"I wasn't aware there was an *us*."

He tossed the gown on the floor and strode forward. His hands were around her waist before she could run for cover. "In the meadow, in the jet, in your house... and before that, in my soul. Yes, there was an *us*. It's still here. I wanted to make it go away. I tried!" He ground out the words. "I can't control what I feel for you, Diane!"

"It must be arduous work, all those beautiful women in your arms, trying to forget me." She raised a brow at him. Humor was her only defense now. If she didn't laugh she would dissolve in tears.

He shook his head violently. "I must have been a different man to see anything in them."

She smiled, pleased despite the bittersweet nature of his compliment. What, after all, did it matter now?

"I'm going," she said softly. "I can't stay here and keep up this pretense of cool civility. I don't think you can, either."

He looked at her, his dark eyes pleading, begging her for another solution while knowing there was none. Slowly, his hands slipped from her waist.

She could think of nothing more to say. She wanted him more than her next breath. Or the one after that. She wanted his body, his heart, his very soul.

"You're not touching me," she murmured, "but I can still feel your hands. It's like that all the time."

He hung his head and closed his eyes. "Every night, I lay awake, aching to come to your room."

"I wish you had," she whispered.

He squinted and looked away from her, as if her brightness hurt his eyes. "It will end when you leave. It has to."

"I know." She drew a slow breath for strength. "You'd better go now."

For a long moment neither of them breathed and neither moved. The world seemed to stand still. Even the distant music fell silent. She could almost hear the castle settling around them, centuries of stone closing them off from the world.

Abruptly Thomas stepped forward and swept her into his arms. He kissed her deeply, devouring her, savoring her—a man bereft of nourishment, desperately trying to replenish himself and store up for the long fast ahead. His hands moved over her, through the cotton nightshirt, reminding himself of favorite places, making her crave again all that he had given her before and more.

He backed her up against one foot post of the bed, and she felt her spine lengthen against the smooth wood, accept its support. Her insides melted as he slipped his hands beneath her nightshirt to shape her bottom. She lifted her knee gently, running it up the inside of his trouser leg, and watched his eyes widen with anticipation as she cautiously nudged him. She could feel the heaviness of him and she pressed a little harder, delighting in his wide-eyed reaction.

Gripping her hand, he guided it beneath the sleek black cummerbund of his tuxedo. Her fingertips met him—hot, long, full. She caressed him, cupped him lovingly, delighted in the glorious weight of him in her palm, ran her hand up him again. She touched the tip of him and smiled, letting him know that she knew how close he was to the edge.

Her smile hadn't fully ripened to a grin before he was pulling off his clothing. She wanted to say something sophisticated, sexy, devil-may-care, but the words wouldn't form on her lips. In the next second he swiftly rid her of her nightshirt.

The room was cool, even in the summer. She gasped softly as the air hit her skin. He smiled and wrapped his body around her. The thick black fur of his chest shaded to less dense patches across his stomach and a reddish nest around his manhood. She couldn't recall a more breathtaking sight. She touched him. Everywhere.

And watched him swell still wider as he took a small foil packet from the pocket of his trousers and handed it to her. She removed the smooth latex disk, and although her hands were shaking, she managed to roll the thin protective layer down over him.

She couldn't imagine how she'd accommodated him the last time. Yet somehow she knew she had. And would again.

Diane gazed questioningly up at Thomas, and the wild look in his eyes softened, tamed by the trust in her eyes.

Slowly he lifted her and, cradling her to him with one arm, he reached down and pulled back the heavy woven bedspread to reveal pristine white sheets. She looped her arms around his muscled neck and held on as he bent to place her in the bed. Smiling down at her, he stretched his body over hers.

"Given the choice," he whispered, "I'd make love to you for the next three hours or until exhaustion. But I'd be missed in the ballroom."

"I suppose so," she murmured, capturing his wonderful eyes with hers as he moved her legs apart with his wide knee.

"I wouldn't want anyone to come looking for me and find us here."

"No," she agreed.

He shifted his hips closer but tested her first with his fingertips.

She arched her back and chuckled low in her throat. "You don't have to worry about my being ready, m'lord. We crossed that bridge a long time ago."

"Good." His voice was gruff with emotion. He brushed himself across the sensitive outer lips of her feminine core.

She let out a whimper. "Don't tease." She was throbbing with hunger for him. "Please, now..."

"As you wish, m'lady."

His slide into her was long and steady and purposeful, his eyes flashing with black fire. She wrapped her arms around his neck and pulled him down to kiss him as she curled her long legs around his hips and brought him deeper still.

Burying his face in the pillows above her shoulder, he smothered a primal bellow of satisfaction, and she took her pleasure along with his.

Seven

Thomas drew Diane close and kissed the top of her head, then her lips, gently parted in slumber. "Stay here," he whispered as she stirred and he reluctantly disentangled himself from her long, silky limbs. He would have given anything to remain beneath the sheets with her, but he'd been gone from the celebration in the ballroom for over an hour. If both of them remained absent for much longer, someone might put one and one together.

"Where're you goin'?" she slurred drowsily.

"To check on Jacob and Allison. As soon as I'm able, I'll come back."

She cracked open one pretty eye. "Maybe I should—"

"Forget it, Sleeping Beauty. I'll make your apologies, if necessary. You told Allison you had a headache, right?"

She nodded and rolled over with a blissful sigh.

Thomas tucked his shirt into his trousers and ran her brush through his hair, smoothing it back from his face, which was still flushed. He didn't know what to do about that. Maybe a few fast waltzes and he could claim his raised color was due to the dancing.

Thomas quietly closed her door behind himself and followed the faint sounds of music and laughter, back through the twisting stone corridors. Many were less stark than they had been two years ago. Allison had left her delicate mark on the crystal palace, brightening the decor, bringing treasured heirlooms out of vaults and into the light of day despite the worried cluckings of insurance underwriters and some of the older members of the court. She was a very popular queen, beloved by the people of Elbia. Jacob had chosen well and happily. Thomas had to admit he'd never seen his young friend so utterly at peace with life as during the days since his marriage.

Thomas stopped beneath the lofty arch that separated the formal dining room from the ballroom and took in the spectacular array of couples dancing to Strauss. The swirl of colors and glittering lights might have been a painting by Degas. But his mind was on other things.

Marriage, he mused. Why did men like his father, who so viciously protected their independence, even bother with the institution? The Earl of Sussex had never been a true father to his sons. Even today the man tolerated only the briefest visits from them. Christopher, the youngest, lived in Scotland now. Matthew, the middle son, had emigrated to the United States, having given up all hope of becoming close to his father or his brothers. And Thomas had found his surrogate family in another country.

He wasn't unhappy with the arrangement, Thomas decided as he watched Jacob and Allison, seated on the dais, their hands clasped lightly as they observed their friends, neighbors and subjects in celebration. The royal family needed and appreciated him, treated him as warmly as if he were Jacob's brother and their children's uncle. But something was missing. Thomas had known that for a while now. Something was definitely missing from his life, though he hadn't been able to put it into words.

Never mind, he thought. All that mattered tonight was getting through the next few hours. After the guests left, he could return to Diane's bed. He thought of his own bed, which had always felt perfectly adequate although no one but he had ever slept in it. He'd never allowed a woman to even enter his room. He changed his own sheets, kept the place scrupulously clean. It had been his sanctuary.

But now that Diane had invaded it, the places she'd walked and things she'd touched would always remind him of her.

Thinking of her in this way, he felt compelled to go to her. Yet he had to stay. He tried to think of ways to make the time pass faster.

The dream became reality sometime in the very early hours of morning. One moment Diane was lying alone in the antique bed in her room. The next, a splendidly naked Thomas was enfolding her in his corded arms, turning her to face him as easily as if she were the single petal of a flower. She felt tiny and vulnerable beside him, but at the same time safe from all harm. Her head was still foggy from sleep, yet she felt every touch of his hands, his mouth, his desire as if her senses were hyper-attuned. She pushed aside all concerns for the future and simply experienced him. And when they had finished making love for the second time that night, he kissed her throat and murmured sweet utterances in her ear as she drifted away.

Never had she been happier.

It was not yet light when he stirred, making her aware of his presence again. His lips closed over hers before she could do more than crack open her eyes. "I need to go," he said. "Before the house awakens."

"I know." Diane sighed and lifted her arms from around his shoulders. But he hesitated. Curious, she reached down and touched him, then giggled. Amazing, she thought. "Have you informed the rest of your body that you're leaving?"

He rolled laughing brown eyes. "It's not listening to reason."

"Will it accept an IOU?"

"With great reluctance."

"Promise it a good time tonight."

He grinned at her. "Come to my room then. You know how to find it?"

"Yes."

He kissed her breasts and she felt a flame reignite within her. But he forced himself off the bed, and a few minutes later, dressed again in his formal wear, his tie hanging loose, tuxedo jacket flung cavalierly over one shoulder, he slipped out her door with a parting wink.

Diane lay in the tangle of mussed linens for another

half hour. She felt deliciously drained of all tension, delightfully lazy. But she was getting hungry, and she knew Cook would have fresh pastries and steaming coffee waiting on the sideboard in the cozy family dining room. The thought of food set her stomach gurgling with anticipation.

"All right, all right," she told it. "I'm up." It took her another twenty minutes to wash and pull on casual, white drawstring pants and a summery pastel jersey. When she walked into the dining room, only Allison was there.

"Good morning," Diane called out cheerfully. It seemed the entire world glowed with a golden aura this morning. Through the expanse of bright glass along one wall she could see the royal gardens. Blossoms in red, blue and pink shot up through waves of green foliage. A burst of lavender wisteria followed a curve of white trellis.

Allison smiled at her. "Is your headache better?"

"Yes, much," Diane said quickly as she tried to choose from among the delectable arrangement of breakfast breads. "I was sorry to miss the rest of the party."

Her sister nodded and took a bite of almond croissant. "We missed you," she murmured after swallowing. "Particularly since you'll be leaving us so soon."

At first the comment didn't make sense to Diane. Then she remembered that only yesterday she had told Allison she would soon be returning to Connecticut. How quickly things changed. This morning she couldn't imagine leaving Elbia, ever. "Maybe I could stay just a while longer," she whispered, and chose a fat cinnamon bun dripping with icing.

"It's difficult, I know," Allison said slowly, "going back to a house you shared with Gary.... And then there's Thomas...."

Her words hung ominously in the air, and Diane swung around to face her. "What does Thomas have to do with whether or not I stay?"

"I'm not sure. Maybe you should tell me." Allison observed her solemnly from across the table.

A chill shot through Diane as if ice water had been pumped into her veins. How had Allison guessed? She quickly poured herself a cup of coffee and sat down. "Neither Gary nor Thomas has any influence over whether I stay or go," she stated crisply.

"Then you're not trying to punish that jerk by taking Thomas as your lover?"

Their eyes met across the table. Diane looked away, horrified, unable to answer her. Was that what she'd been doing? Please, it had to be more than that!

"You see, I—" Allison brushed her long, blond hair out of her eyes and closed her hands around her coffee cup but did not drink. "—I saw Thomas leaving your bedroom this morning."

Diane felt her cheeks radiate white-hot. She couldn't lie to her sister, but she couldn't very well tell her the truth, either. Allison was loyal to her, but she would never keep secrets from Jacob.

"I...I don't know what to say," Diane whispered.

Allison stared into her coffee. "He's a wonderful man, Thomas. A kind, generous, fiercely protective friend and ally to Jacob, and to me and the children. We all love him dearly."

"I know," Diane said.

"I don't want to see him hurt. But—" she held up a hand when Diane opened her mouth to protest "—I know you wouldn't intentionally do anything to harm him. It's you I'm more worried about.''

Diane reached for the bun on her plate. Although her stomach was churning, she needed something to keep her hands busy. She tore off a bit and forced it into her mouth, chewed and swallowed without tasting it. "I can take care of myself."

"I'm sure you can, if you have all the information needed to make a sensible decision."

"What do you mean by that?"

"I mean, you don't know Thomas very well, but Jacob's very close to him, and we've talked about him a lot."

"So fill me in." Diane's skin prickled with anticipation. She was hungry to learn all she could of the man who had introduced her to passion.

"You realize he's not just a royal flunky."

"Son of a British earl, yes."

"Exactly. And an aristocrat in his own right—the Earl of Chichester, who will become Earl of Sussex when his father dies. Did you also know he is one of the wealthiest men in England?"

Diane stared at her sister. "He works for Jacob. I figured he needed a job to support himself."

Allison shook her head slowly. "When Thomas turned twenty-one, his father gave him his inheritance. Something in the six figure-area, according to Jacob. The Earl told him to do with it as he would. I gather the money was awarded less out of love than as a means of cutting the few ties that remained between them. Goodbye, so long, have a good life—that sort of thing."

Diane was astounded. "How cold!"

"To us, yes. Apparently, Thomas hadn't expected

anything more from his father. At that time he was in the British Army, training in an elite commando squad. He had no need for money and, disdaining his father's gift, he invested most of it in a fledgling computer company that became one of the most successful businesses in the world.''

Diane began to get the picture. "Oh my," she said, exhaling. "But I don't understand. Why does Thomas work at all?''

Allison shrugged. "He seems to have been looking for a place to belong, and he found it with the von Austerands. But basically he's a loner. Always will be, I suspect.''

"He has a social life. He dates.''

"Oh, yes. He does like the ladies." Allison laughed. "But he never mixes business or his professional life with his holiday trips. Most of the women we never even see. A few are allowed to attend a palace function, but there's rarely a return visit." Allison fixed her with a meaningful look.

"You're afraid he'll dump me?''

"I just think you should be aware that he's not the type of man who sticks around for long or changes for a woman.''

"Jacob changed," Diane pointed out. "He was the ultimate playboy.''

Allison smiled. "Yes, and I'll be forever thankful he reformed himself for me and for Cray. But you can't count on that happening with Thomas. He's been a bachelor all of his forty years. That's a long time to establish habits.''

Diane thought about Thomas's reluctance to let their affair become public. "How would Jacob feel about my sleeping with his chief advisor?''

Allison's face darkened. "That's the other issue I wanted to talk to you about. He tolerates Thomas's discreet liaisons because of his own past, I suspect, but also because they never involve the inner circle here at court and never interfere with our work. A lot of business gets done in short order here, and Thomas is on call twenty-four hours a day. Jacob depends upon him implicitly."

"I see."

"There's more. Although we employ married couples, affairs among the staff might enable political intrigue. Elbia's a small country, but it's allied to many larger ones and we are privy to secret information. Jacob has dismissed offenders in the past whose indiscretions threatened either our neighbors' security or ours. As a show of impartiality he might ask for Thomas's resignation if he thought you two—"

"Enough," Diane said weakly, "I understand." And so did Thomas, she realized now. This was why he'd been so cautious about allowing himself to become intimate with her. But what either of them could do about it now, she didn't know. She hurt inside when she thought about giving him up. "Will you give us a few days to work things out before you say anything to Jacob?"

Allison smiled softly. "I can do that." She reached across and touched her sister's arm. "I'm sorry. I wish I could do or say something to make this easier. I'd have warned you sooner, but I couldn't have guessed. You and Thomas—" She shrugged.

"I know," Diane admitted. "It took me by surprise, too."

* * *

The days that followed were as bittersweet as the rich Schokoladetortes sold in the bakery in the town below the castle. Diane spent as much time with Thomas as possible. Whenever he could excuse himself from work, he would seek her out in the garden, the private rooms of the castle, or the village. He had a knack for knowing where she would be at any given time, although she often wandered across the grounds or through the shop-lined streets without announcing her destination to anyone.

Each night they made love. Diane wondered how she'd ever slept alone, and before that how she'd slept with a man she didn't love. She became addicted to a new sleeping position. She curled into Thomas's chest, placed her cheek on the muscled pad over his heart, nestled her lips against the soft mat of dark hair, crooked her knee to angle her leg over his hips. Lying with him beneath the cool sheets, she slept so blissfully and deeply she was amazed to be able to wake the next morning.

Yet, in the back of her mind, Diane knew time was working against them. Soon Allison would feel obligated to inform Jacob of their affair. Before that time came she must tell Thomas that Allison knew their secret. Then he would decide whether to go to Jacob himself or break off with her. With each hour that passed, she told herself she shouldn't put off leaving for home any longer. But it was hard to let go of happiness when it had been so long in coming.

One day, nearly a week after the grand ball, Thomas found her alone in the family dining room and, after looking around to make sure no one was watching, kissed her softly on the cheek. "There is a telephone call for you. Jacob sent me to find you. It's your mother."

"The children...has something happened—"

"Don't panic." Thomas smiled reassuringly at her. "Jacob spoke with her. He says it sounds like good news, although he didn't explain what that meant."

The stab of tension immediately felt less severe. Good news? She couldn't imagine what that meant. Unless little Gare had finally learned to put his face in the water while swimming. His brother and sister had been working with him all last summer, but he'd still been terrified.

"Are you eating lunch now?" she asked.

"I was going to." He looped his strong arms around her waist. "Unless you have a better suggestion."

She laughed at him. "I'll go see what's up in Florida, then be back to eat with you, wicked man."

She dashed out of the room, still tingling from the devilish twinkle in his dark eyes. The stairs to the floor above, where Jacob's office was located, were cut from native stone and twisted around a central column of gargoylelike creatures in whimsical poses. She thought how much her children would love exploring the endless corridors and the dozens of rooms with secret passages leading between them.

Jacob looked up when she knocked. He waved her in, seeming relieved to hand the receiver over to her. "Yes, Mrs. Fields, she's here now. I'll say goodbye for the time being. Good health to you, too."

Diane covered the receiver quickly. "She talked your ear off, didn't she?"

Jacob shrugged good-naturedly as if to say, "What else would you expect of a mother-in-law?"

"Hi, Mom," Diane said, laughing to herself. Leave it to her mother to tie up a king with mundane news from home. "How are the kids?"

"Oh, they're having a marvelous time, just marvelous. In a way I hate to see their visit end so soon, but I know it's for the best."

"End?" Diane echoed.

"Why, yes, hasn't Gary called you yet?"

"N-n-n-o," she said slowly. It felt as if a noxious vapor was seeping into her lungs with each breath—burning her from the inside out. "Why should he call me?"

"Well, I thought…I mean, when he asked for you and I told him you were in Europe with your sister…"

"Why did he call?" Diane asked, fighting for control.

"Well, from the way he was talking, I had the feeling he wanted to get back together with you."

"He *what?*" She didn't believe it for a minute. Her mother must be insane.

"Well, he is the father of your children. I'm sure it's possible he's had a change of heart and is willing to put the past behind him."

"I doubt the man could have a change of heart, since he never had one to begin with."

"Now, Diane, dear, I know it's not easy to leave the bitterness behind, but—"

"But nothing, Mother!" she snapped, despite her intention to remain calm. "The man is incapable of honest emotion, at least toward me. You must have read a lot into whatever he said."

"But don't you want to be a family again?" her mother asked.

That did it. All the guilt, all the disappointment and heartache and emptiness washed back over her. "A family," she said slowly, "does not require the presence of a man like Gary Fields. We will do just fine without him."

As she hung up the phone a few moments later, it was clear to Diane that although her mother meant well, she didn't have a clue how impossible living with Gary had been. It was certainly all the more clear to Diane herself, now that she'd learned what being with a real man could be like. Thomas made her laugh, made her happy just to be alive. He encouraged her dreams instead of crushing them. He excited her to heights she'd never believed possible, and he satisfied her every longing.

But she couldn't explain any of that to her parents. They'd be appalled. Diane sighed.

Jacob looked up at her. "I'm sorry. I should have left the room and given you some privacy."

She waved off his concern. "Never mind, it was another of my mother's attempts to deny my divorce."

"You don't think Gary called her?"

"Oh, I have no doubt he did call." Her sudden, brittle laugh was without humor. "*Why* he called, that's the question. I can't believe that after nearly a year of separation, he suddenly wants to return to married life."

"He's finally come to his senses?"

"What senses?" she groaned.

Someone knocked at the half-open door.

"Yes," Jacob said.

Thomas stepped into the room. "Will you be having lunch with the family, sir, or should I bring you a tray?''

Although he was questioning Jacob, his eyes strayed toward Diane.

''I'll be right down,'' Jacob said, then turned back to her. ''So what will you do if your mother is right and Gary does want to reconcile?''

Thomas's expression gave away nothing, but she felt a tremor pass through the air between them. ''I'll tell him to go fly a kite.''

Jacob nodded. ''I don't blame you. The odds of his reforming at this point aren't good. But if you do decide to leave early, just let me know and I'll have Thomas make the necessary arrangements.''

''Thank you.'' She turned and, still feeling Thomas's eyes on her, left the room. She was halfway down the long hallway before he caught up with her.

''What's going on?'' he asked.

She shook her head. ''Nothing. At least nothing that concerns us.''

''It didn't sound that way to me.'' His voice was strained, his eyes dark and troubled. ''Jacob said something about your ex wanting to reconcile. I assume that means he wants to come home to you and the children.''

''What Gary wants no longer matters,'' she said firmly.

Thomas studied her expression as they walked. She had a sense of him holding his breath. He reached out and brushed the backs of his fingers along her cheek. ''Is that really true?''

''Of course it's true!'' She stopped and swung around to face him. ''I told you, I don't love the man.''

"Even so, you may not be thinking this through clearly."

Her irritation turned to pure fury. How dare he presume to tell her what or how she should be thinking! Her cheeks pinked, hot with rage, but he apparently didn't notice.

"You need to look at the big picture," he continued. "You and I, we're all wrapped up in physical reactions, in a…an…" He hesitated.

"An affair?" she filled in the word he hadn't wanted to say. "Is that all this has been for you? One of many short-lived, provocative interludes in your life?" She felt as if her skin was throwing sparks. Her eyes were hot and stinging. Her bottom lip quivered traitorously. "You're about to tell me to go back to him, aren't you?"

Thomas took a deep breath and let it out slowly. "I'm just encouraging you to slow down and think about what you are doing…what *we* are doing. What's best for the children, and for you in the long run? That's the important thing."

She backed away from him, struck cold by his words. "No, you're not thinking about me or my kids. You're looking for an escape hatch."

"That's not true, Diane!"

"It is," she murmured dully, and started to turn away.

An iron grip around her upper arm stopped her and swung her back to face him. Suddenly he had her in his arms, trapped against his massive chest. She struggled, but he only tightened his hold.

"Listen to me!" he growled. "This isn't the way I want it to be, either, but you were leaving in a few weeks anyway, right? That's what we'd agreed. The very most we could have would be the summer. Then you were returning to Connecticut to be with your children and start a new life. Isn't that so?''

When she didn't immediately answer, he gave her a little shake. She cleared the thickness from her throat and rasped, ''Yes!''

''Gary may be a fool for neglecting you, then leaving you for another woman, but he is your children's father. If there's any chance that he might change and—''

''No!'' she shouted.

''Listen!'' He shook her harder. ''I know you're a strong woman and could make it on your own. But children need a father, and it seems he wants to try to be there for all of you. You know I can never marry you and become something I'm not. If I thought there was even a chance, don't you think I'd try?''

She couldn't endure looking him in the eyes any longer. ''I...I don't know,'' she sobbed. ''Thomas, let me go.''

''It's for the best,'' he murmured dully.

''No,'' she whispered. ''No, it's not.''

Slowly his grip loosened and she felt the blood rush back into her arms with a heavy throb. She felt dizzy and weak and wanted desperately to lean on him, but showing emotional frailty now would buy her nothing. She sensed his determination to let her go, forever, and that hurt more than she could ever say. He was willing to give her away to another man, without a fight, without even blinking.

She stepped back from him, turned and set her shoulders, then held her chin high and walked away.

Eight

Thomas felt as if the weight of the universe had settled upon his shoulders. Telling Diane she should go home to a man she didn't love, telling her it was best for everyone concerned, had been the most difficult thing he'd ever done. But did he have any choice?

Gary apparently hadn't been much of a husband to Diane, but they had a history that included three children. He, Thomas, could satisfy her in bed and afford to give her luxuries. But how long would it be before he'd succumb to his fate and walk out of her life, leaving her shattered? Giving up Diane was the right thing to do, he told himself for the hundredth time. She must return to her own world, and he must rededicate himself to the life he'd chosen with his royal family.

Nevertheless, guilt still gnawed at him. Every time he was alone in a room with Jacob, he felt himself tense. He'd never been anything but absolutely honest with the young man who had become king. And so, that evening, while the two of them were working alone in Jacob's office, Thomas turned to him.

"There is something you need to know, Your Highness."

Jacob didn't look up from the wide, elegantly carved desk, but a shadow of a smile lifted his lips. "This sounds serious. Have you knocked up a contessa?" His unexpected humor made the job all the harder.

"No, sir. It's far worse, I'm afraid."

Lifting his head slowly, Jacob studied his friend's solemn expression. "Hard to imagine. You're feeling well, aren't you? It's not a health problem, I hope."

"Nothing like that, sir." To the contrary, until that bloody phone call, he'd never felt stronger, younger, more alive in his life! Being with Diane had given him all that and more. "But I have done something terrible. It's fully my fault and in no way should what I'm about to tell you reflect on your sister-in-law."

Jacob's features went suddenly wooden. "What has Diane done that you have to protect her?"

Thomas was horrified. "She's done nothing but be herself, let me assure you. I…we—" He scrambled desperately for words. "No one planned to have this happen. I admit to having been attracted to her since we first met, and apparently she found me moderately acceptable. When you sent me to the States to determine if something was wrong—"

"Stop!" Jacob shouted.

Thomas stiffened his spine, closed his mouth and waited for the worst.

The young king stood up from his desk and turned

to face the window overlooking the dark garden. Only then did Thomas see the two women outside, Diane and Allison, sitting on a stone bench in the moonlight, their heads lowered in conversation. Neither appeared very happy. Perhaps, he thought with a tinge of irony, they are having this same conversation.

"If you're about to tell me that you have been sleeping with my wife's sister—"

"Sir, I assure you, it wasn't a careless affair." Thomas fought off the overwhelming panic. This was not going at all well. He had to keep a clear head and explain the confusing, complex turn of events.

"What was it, then?" Jacob shouted, spinning toward him. "Are you telling me you considered the consequences, *then* decided sleeping with my wife's sister made sense?"

"No, I mean, yes, but—"

"What were you thinking, man? She's been through enough!" Jacob glared at him. "The hope was Diane would come here, relax and regain her strength, then go home and be able to better deal with her life."

"I know, yes, of course…" How could he argue with that?

"I would have given her a generous allowance and supported all four of them, of course, but she's a proud woman and won't accept charity."

"Yes, sir, I know."

"She was vulnerable. You should have considered her your very last target, Lothario."

Thomas nodded sadly. Hadn't he known it all along? Hadn't he understood, too, how angry Jacob would be? And now as he heard the cutting edge of the king's voice and saw the fire in his blue eyes, he remembered that Jacob was not a man to be crossed, even by a friend.

But he'd still rather confess his transgressions than try to hide them.

"I don't suppose you ever offered to marry the woman?" the king asked.

Thomas looked up, surprised that Jacob would even ask. "No, sir. That wasn't considered an option. Our lives are too different."

"She was willing to have sex with you and expected nothing in return? No future?"

He couldn't answer. Not in a way that would satisfy Jacob or make himself feel any better about what he'd done. "We both understood it was a temporary arrangement. I didn't seduce her, if that's what you're thinking. We both wanted—"

"Yes, yes. I understand the power of lust well enough."

Thomas had no doubt he did. Jacob had sampled his own generous share of the female population on several continents as a young man. He'd been perfectly satisfied with his playboy, bachelor life until he discovered he'd fathered a young son by the American woman he'd shared a summer fling with. It had taken the petite blonde commoner to tame him.

But he wouldn't remind Jacob of those traumatic days, just as he hoped this time would pass and someday Jacob would pardon him for what he'd done. Just as he hoped Diane would come to forgive him for letting her go.

"I think you'd better arrange for Mrs. Fields's return to Connecticut," Jacob said stiffly.

"Yes, sir. I believe that's what she wants now, too."

"Fine. Do it."

"Sir, I only meant to help her—"

"Spare me," Jacob bit off. "You were thinking with your—" He stopped himself and growled. "Leave. Make the arrangements."

Thomas had never felt so small in his life. He felt physically, morally and emotionally insignificant. A slug, a worm, a lowly one-celled parasite...not a man. If he had exerted any amount of willpower and common sense instead of letting his hormones run amok, he wouldn't have touched Diane. The problem was, she'd been so eager, so lovely, so tempting in every way, and he'd felt the urgency of her need for a man.

How could he not respond to the woman?

No, he corrected himself, she was far more than a needy female. She was unique and precious in his experience. If he'd been able to stay with anyone, it would have been her. But human nature and blood would tell.

"Yes, sir," he murmured, sinking fast in his despair. "I'll make arrangements with your pilot."

"And you'll leave her alone from now on. Is that understood?" The expression on Jacob's face demanded allegiance.

"Understood perfectly, Your Highness."

The day Diane left Elbia was the saddest of her life. As she settled herself into the leather cushions on the von Austerand jet, she chided herself on having been so naive. A woman who'd been married and given birth to three children should know more about the ways of men and women. But perhaps, in all fairness, an early marriage and her quiet lifestyle had sheltered her. Other, more experienced women no doubt took new relationships with men and the sub-sequent break-ups much more in stride.

Thomas's desertion stung bitterly. She felt his loss as physical pain—an aching in her heart, a hard knot in her stomach. Her eyes burned with unshed tears. Only as the jet took flight, rushing up into the blue July skies over the snow-tipped mountains surrounding Elbia, did she realize she had believed in her heart they might find a way to stay together.

In the days that followed, Diane tried to reorient herself to the world she was familiar with. Nanticoke was a beautiful, picture-book-quaint New England town, built around a white-steepled church and village green, with a bandstand for summer concerts and a cannon to memorialize the town's Revolutionary War patriots. She had always loved it, always felt comfortable here. It was where she and Allison had played as children, and where she'd always imagined herself living.

Until she'd spent a month in Elbia. Until a magnificent bear of a man had taught her what it was like to be swept away by a passionate love.

She knew now, of course, that he'd never truly loved her. His tenderness and desire must have been part of a mating ritual to him. He'd had plenty of women before her, would have others in her wake. He was a loner, loyal only to Jacob. As soon as Thomas had seen the opportunity for conveniently moving her out of his life, he'd jumped at it.

She walked around her house, trying to focus on the future. It would be another week before the children returned; her mother had asked that they be allowed to stay with her in Florida a little longer. Everything felt small, cramped, plain after the soaring stone walls and antiques-filled rooms of the castle. She recalled the ballroom on the night of the grand ball, with its swirling couples, and wished she'd had a chance to waltz with Thomas…but almost immediately was glad she hadn't. It would be just one more memory to struggle to forget.

She drank gallons of herb tea and tried again and again to think about her future, but felt all the more lost. At night she lay in bed, stared at the ceiling, and the tears came no matter how hard she fought them. Thomas obviously didn't care that she'd left, but she missed him fiercely.

Finally Diane got up enough energy to begin her job search. She responded to several ads and made appointments for interviews. She caught up with housework and bills that had accumulated during her absence. Her mother called twice and asked if she'd heard yet from Gary.

"No," Diane snapped. "Not one word." Her fervent hope was that her mother had somehow misinterpreted his call and he'd only been curious as to the children's well-being.

"That's odd," Margaret Fields mused. "He seemed so anxious to reach you. I do hope you won't be rude to him when he does call."

"Mother…"

"Well, you can be very short at times, Diane."

She didn't feel like pointing out that being curt with the husband who'd abandoned her and their children for a teenage receptionist wasn't exactly an overreaction.

"I have things to do, Mother. I'll talk with you soon. Give my love to the children."

She thought about jobs again that night and remembered speaking with Allison in the garden the day before she left Elbia. Her sister had brought up examples of the royal family's charitable works around the world. "Consider joining our international staff," Allison had said. "I know you'd do a wonderful job and you'd love it."

At the time, Diane had thought Allison was just trying to find another excuse for giving her money. But now she wondered if she'd too hastily dismissed a legitimate job offer and what was certain to be a better lifestyle for her children. On the other hand, working on her sister's special programs would mean living much of the year in Elbia and seeing Thomas nearly every day. She couldn't bear that, loving him as she did.

She put that possibility out of her mind. Very firmly out of her mind, and hit the local classifieds again. While waiting for something better to come along, she took a temporary job at the local grocery store to make sure she didn't fall behind on the bills.

When the children returned home, she scheduled her work hours so that Elly could watch them while she was at the store. Then one Saturday as she looked out her kitchen window, she saw a man standing in her backyard, watching her children play.

For a fleeting second she thought—Thomas!

But it wasn't him. This man was a good foot shorter and inches narrower at the shoulders. What was a stranger doing in her yard?

Her protective instincts kicking in, Diane raced out her kitchen door, down the cement steps and through the gate into the backyard. Before she reached him, she knew who it was.

"What are you doing here, Gary?"

He turned and grinned at her, as if she ought to be pleased to see him. "Hey, there, Di. The kids look great! All tanned and healthy from that Florida sunshine."

"Answer me, dammit. Why are you here?"

He flung an arm around her shoulders. She didn't even waste the energy to shrug it off. "So I hear from your mom that you've had a vacation, too. That's great. You deserve a break. Did Prince Charming treat you like a poor cousin or did he at least pretend you were part of the family?"

"Jacob is King of Elbia now," she corrected him. "He's a gracious, warm man, a good father and loving husband."

Gary laughed. "Guess he can afford to be, with the millions he's got."

"Why are you here?" she persisted. She wasn't going to bring up her mother's theory of his wanting to get back together with her. Let him just dare to even hint at it.

"To see my kids, of course. Don't you think I miss 'em?"

"You never did before."

His smile left to be replaced by an exaggerated stage frown. "You're right. You're absolutely right, Di. I didn't know what I was missing. Shoulda spent more time with them."

The two boys called to him from the slide beside the swings. "Hey, Dad, look at this!"

They were showing off for him, trying to hold his attention by attempting daredevil, headfirst descents of the steep metal slope. Gary waved in their direction, but almost immediately turned back to Diane.

"The thing is," he said, lowering his head to nearly

touch foreheads with her, "I feel real bad about walking out and leaving you holding the bag and all. Kids are expensive."

"Children need to be taken care of. The money is beside the point."

"Well, yeah…but it costs to feed 'em and buy shoes and all. Anyway, I've been thinking. It ain't fair that I'm not helping support them." He held up a hand in protest against an objection she hadn't given. "No, no. I realize we signed papers, all legal and proper, and you like to handle things on your own. But it's only right I do my share."

She stared at him. Something definitely was wrong with the man. The only share he'd ever wanted to protect was his own time away from the house, hanging out with his friends at the local bar. At least, that was where she'd thought he'd been.

"What do you see as your share?" she asked suspiciously.

"Well, that depends."

She raised one eyebrow skeptically. "On what?"

"See money is a little tight just now. Me and Darlene, we've been cutting the corners best we can. But I'm trying to start my own construction business, and every damn bank I go to, they want collateral for a loan, and it's not like I have any since you kept the house."

Fear rushed through her. "You are *not* taking this house from us."

"Wasn't suggesting such a thing, believe me!" He looked astonished.

"Then what are you suggesting, Gary?"

He kissed her on the nose—a gesture she'd always hated because it meant he felt guilty about something he'd done or was about to do. "All I need is a little start-up cash, Di. Just twenty or thirty thou. Once the business gets rolling, I'll be able to give you plenty, like clockwork, every month."

"I have no money to give you, and you know that," she ground out before the wily glimmer in his eyes tipped her off. "You're not thinking of asking Jacob for money!"

"'Course not. I was going to ask you to ask him."

She slipped out from under his arm. "Forget it."

"But, Di…be reasonable. We're all family, right? You and me, we may have split up, but he's still your brother-in-law, and I was his brother-in-law, and it's only reasonable that—"

"No!" she shouted. She was aware that the children had stopped what they were doing to watch them. She hated arguing in front of them, but there was no way she would have any part of Gary's con games. He was a decent worker under a good supervisor, but he didn't have it in him to run a company. No matter how much money Jacob or a bank might give him, he'd blow it within six months.

Gary stared at her. "I mean it. I'll give you some money for the little beasties as soon as I start turning a profit."

One thing she had to give him—he had nerve. "Visit with the children as long as you like, Gary." She turned back toward the house. "But don't expect any handouts from me or Jacob. You and Darlene will just have to make it on your own."

Thomas didn't get out of the car. After almost two weeks of fantasizing about Diane, he had given in to his need to see her. When Jacob mentioned a problem with the New York branch of the Von Austerand Relief Program, he volunteered to make the trip. They hadn't mentioned Diane, but Jacob had hesitated before agreeing that Thomas should go in his stead to the States.

The day he left, Jacob took him aside and they smoked a cigar in his private study. "I know what you're thinking. You're wondering if you can see her while you're there."

Thomas nodded. "Believe me, if I could put the woman from my mind, I would."

"Then she is different from the others," Jacob observed.

"As night and day." Thomas sighed. "But I won't do anything to hurt her again. If I see her at all, it will only be to make sure she's safe and doesn't need anything."

Jacob nodded. "I'm sorry I was so angry with you the other day. You took me by surprise."

"I know."

Jacob puffed thoughtfully. "Are you sure you don't want to marry the woman?"

"It's not a matter of wanting something, it's a matter of who I am."

"And do you know who you are?"

Thomas stared at him. It seemed a strange question.

"Never mind," Jacob said with a wave of his cigar. "You have a right to a private life. I just don't want to see either of you hurt. You're two of my favorite people. Be careful, old friend."

Thomas had told himself he would be careful. He would simply do as he'd done before, only with the foreknowledge of the possible traps laid for his heart. He would just stop by Diane's house to make sure she'd found a job and see if she'd reconciled with Gary. As soon as he was assured she was all right, he would leave. If he could have gotten a straight answer out of her over the telephone, he'd have called. But he feared she would hang up on him.

He pulled up in front of her house. Her car was in the driveway, and a pickup truck was parked out front. A queer, sour feeling bubbled up inside of him. He moved the rented Lincoln slowly along the street. At last he could see down her driveway to the back-yard. The children were playing boisterously, and a couple stood close together, watching them. The man was only an inch or so taller than the woman. He was speaking intently to her, his arm around her. It was Diane. He knew the subtle curves of her body, the way her dark hair fell almost to her shoulders then curled softly under, the delightful tilt of her hips.

Then the man leaned in front of her and kissed her.

Thomas felt his entire body go rigid. His fingers spasmed on the steering wheel, and he had to stop himself from exploding from the car and racing across cement to tear the man away from her. He closed his eyes and slowly mastered his roiling emotions.

Why was he surprised? Hadn't he advised her to take Gary back? He cursed himself. No other man should be allowed to take her in his arms, ever. Just as no other woman should ever come to his, Thomas's, bed. But all the wishes in the world had come too late.

He jammed his foot on the accelerator, headed for the thruway and didn't let up until he hit the traffic of downtown Manhattan an hour later.

It took the better part of two weeks to rectify the problem with the royal charities. Funds had been appropriated to aid refugee children from the most recent political strife in the Middle East. Somehow, the medical and food supplies that were supposed to be purchased hadn't been. Thomas hired a crack accounting firm. Within a few days they discovered a trail of cash flowing straight into the pockets of an executive Jacob had hired a year earlier.

Most of the money was recovered within twenty-four hours of Thomas confronting the man. He'd stood the bastard up against a wall of windows and told him what he thought ought to be done to a man who took food from the mouths of children. They were fifteen floors above the asphalt of Fifth Avenue, and apparently the fellow took the implied threat seriously.

Which left Thomas free to return to Europe the next day.

But he couldn't stop thinking about Diane. He didn't sleep that night.

At five the next morning he found himself walking the beach at Nanticoke, looking out at a gray dawn over Long Island Sound. It had rained overnight, and the sand was wet. Gulls picked at the flotsam that had been washed up in the dark. He felt hopeless, alone, adrift.

A single figure appeared at the far end of the beach. He could tell it was a woman from the stride and the pale outline of a ponytail swinging behind her head as she ran. Elly Shapiro, the baby-sitter who had taken the children to Florida. She tilted her head to one side as she approached, then smiled when she recognized him.

"You out for exercise, too?" she puffed, jogging in place.

"Just a short stroll," he said. "I'm sorry your time in Florida got cut short, Elly."

"Oh, it's okay. Thank you for paying me my full salary for just half the summer. I got another job when I came home. Dad says my college fund is looking great!" She grinned but continued hopping from foot to foot.

"How are Mrs. Fields and the children?"

"Pretty good, I guess," Elly said. She giggled. "She sure can get steamed."

"Steamed?" he echoed.

"Yeah, you know…she's got a temper. Not at me, of course."

Thomas assumed she was talking about the effect he'd had on her. "Yes, of course."

"You didn't hear?" Elly asked, her pretty green eyes wide and full of delight at a chance to gossip.

"About the Fields getting back together?" he said morbidly.

"No, silly. Mr. Fields came by one day, pretending he was all jazzed about seeing his kids again. But he was really trying to blackmail Mrs. Fields," she whispered in a conspiratorial voice.

Blackmail her? Thomas scowled. Either the girl had a strange imagination or Gary Fields was worse than the typical philandering husband.

He rested his hands on the teenager's shoulders to bring her jogging to a stop. "Elly, what are you talking about?"

"Mr. Fields came to the house, and her oldest boy told me exactly what his father said. He wants to start a business and he was asking Mrs. Fields for money, like umpteen thousand dollars, and she said she didn't have it, and he said she could get it from the king, since he's so rich, and Mrs. Fields told him to get lost!'' She finished her story with a satisfied grin. ''Isn't that cool?''

Thomas released the girl and smiled down at her. His heart suddenly felt lighter. ''Yes, cool indeed.''

Nine

Diane finished giving the children their breakfast and had just sent them off to get dressed when the doorbell rang. She glanced at the clock. It wasn't yet seven. The other children in the neighborhood didn't usually come around quite so early. Frowning, she peeked out the window in the kitchen door to see Elly in her pink warm-up suit.

"Hi, Mrs. Fields. We thought we'd give you a break," Elly said cheerfully when Diane opened the door.

We? she thought. Then she saw the tall figure behind her. Thomas.

She shot him a cold look. "We're doing just fine, Elly. Why don't you come back around noon, as we'd planned."

Thomas shook his head at the teenager, then turned to Diane. "Let her take the children down to the beach for the morning,'' he said, stepping through the door despite Diane's attempt to block his way. ''It's my treat.''

''Did Jacob send you again?'' She would definitely have a word with her brother-in-law about his meddling.

''In a manner of speaking, yes. But this wasn't his or my intended destination.''

She groaned. ''Just leave. We're not going through this again.''

Thomas ignored her. ''Elly, do you know where the children's beach towels and bathing suits are?''

''Yes, sir,'' the teenager said brightly.

''Then why don't you get them changed and hit the beach.'' He pulled a couple bills from his pocket. ''Here's something for snacks, if they get hungry.''

Diane stared at him, aghast. ''Listen. I don't want your help. We're doing just fine.''

He watched Elly disappear into the living room. A second later three squealing voices exuberantly welcomed her. Thomas turned back to face Diane. ''I understand you and Gary aren't getting back together.''

''Which is what I said when I left Elbia.''

''Yes, I know, but—'' he hesitated ''—I thought you might have, anyway.''

''Not while there's warmth in this body.''

He smiled. ''Fair enough. Elly tells me you have a job.''

''That's right…and a good one,'' she said with emphasis. ''I have health benefits, paid vacation, the works.''

''And minimum wage?''

She scowled at him. "My income is my business, no one else's."

"Is it enough to make your mortgage payments and buy food for four?"

She drew in a sharp breath and was about to spout a few choice words she never used in front of the children, but they trooped across the kitchen, carrying their favorite beach toys.

"We're off!" Elly proclaimed, giving Thomas a conspiratorial wink as she marched her charges out the door.

As soon as it closed behind them, Diane rounded on Thomas. "You have no right barging into my home, ordering my children about and criticizing my job choices!"

He smiled complacently down at her. "I'm your friend, Diane. Won't you let me help you?"

She shook her head at him, so angry she was unable to speak. The worst part of it was, even as she ached to clamp her hands around his muscled neck and choke the life out of him, she felt overpowered by his presence. She'd forgotten, or at least tried to forget, how easily he filled a room and made every other object in it seem inconsequential, a miniature of before. His dark eyes fixed on hers, and she found she couldn't look away.

"I don't think we can be just friends, Thomas."

"No?"

"No."

"Why not?"

"Because…because…" Because, she wanted to shout, I'm in love with you, you idiot, and I can't deal with your not loving me! "It just won't work."

"Because we've slept together?"

"That certainly has something to do with it. Now, will you please leave?"

She started to turn away, but he overtook her in two easy strides and turned her round to face him. His expression was stormy, threatening, black. He looked frustrated that she wouldn't listen to him, then something else crossed his face that was far more frightening to her.

"Don't...oh, Thomas," she cried, "don't even think about that!"

He didn't speak, only gazed longingly into her eyes, struggling against some unseen force. With quiet resolution, he lowered his mouth and captured her lips in a kiss that seemed to never end.

Diane opened her lips and savored him. How she'd missed this man!

"I've missed you," he said, miraculously echoing her own thoughts.

She nodded, incapable of speaking.

"Let's not give up yet," he said, his voice gravel rough with emotion. "I was thinking...maybe a long-distance relationship? I'll come whenever I can. I'll tell Jacob and assure him and your sister that I'll take care of you in every possible way. It will be almost as if we're married."

"Almost," she murmured numbly.

"You won't have to work at all, unless you want to," he promised. "Let me take care of the bills. I'll buy you a bigger house, anywhere you like."

She sighed. "Sounds as if you're offering to make me a kept woman."

"I don't mean it like that. You know it."

She took a moment to think about what he'd said, but his words couldn't change what she knew was true. "I would never be comfortable with an arrangement like that. A long-term affair with a man who doesn't love me?"

She looked up questioningly into his deep brown eyes, hoping for the sign she needed, the words that would make everything all right for them. He didn't say them. Three simple words, and he couldn't say them to her. Her world hit bottom.

"I'm sorry, Diane. I've told you who I am."

"I know." She pushed herself up, stood unsteadily, then walked to the kitchen counter and held on. They'd come so close to returning to where they'd been—a passionate limbo where neither her heart nor her soul could rest comfortably. But it seemed to be as much as he was able or willing to give her. "You'd better leave now," she whispered, turning away from him.

Although the next two months were a challenge, Diane managed to function during the days. She continued interviewing for corporate positions and even got a few offers. But in the end she turned those down because they required a long commute and extended work hours, and she couldn't justify leaving her children for so much of every week. Instead, she threw herself into her job at the grocery store, and it wasn't long before her energy was noticed. She was moved up into an assistant manager's position, which meant more money and better benefits.

The nights were the difficult times. Loneliness hurt all the more fiercely after having known Thomas. There was no one to share her days' small triumphs or disasters with. She spoke with Allison at least once a week, and she sensed that although there might be news of Thomas, her sister was being careful not to mention his name. Diane didn't ask about him.

It was near the end of September when she first became suspicious. Her usual feminine cycles had always been unpredictable. So she ignored her body's shenanigans all summer until it occurred to her one autumn afternoon that she hadn't had anything close to a real period for nearly three months.

But surely, this couldn't mean she was... Absolutely not! She'd been with no one other than Thomas...and they'd always used protection. At least, she was pretty sure he'd always—No, wait, she thought, her stomach knotting at the cloudy memory of a day in a sunny meadow. There was that one time. The first time she and Thomas had made love. But he'd removed himself before he'd—

Or at least she'd thought he had left her in time!

What if...?

She didn't dare think of it. But she had heard that no method of birth control, especially that one, was foolproof.

The next day Diane carefully selected a test kit from the pharmacy. During her break, she used the first strip. It came out positive. She told herself it was a fluke and tried the second in the packet. Positive.

Her heart pounded in her chest all afternoon. Sometimes she felt as if she couldn't breathe. She brought the third strip home with her and tested one final time after the children were in bed.

Sighing, she sat on the edge of the bathtub and stared at the colored scrap. No longer could she deny the results. She touched her breasts, and they felt tender, full. She closed her eyes and thought to herself, Well, that's it, then... But strangely enough she didn't feel sad. Yes, there would be another child. But she'd always loved the months of growing a baby inside of her. And this would be a special child. Thomas's baby. Somehow, she'd manage.

"You have a telephone call from Frau Fields, in the United States," Jacob's secretary informed Thomas over the intercom in crisp German.

Thomas's heart gave a lurch. He counted to three to make sure his voice didn't come out as a pitiful squeak. "Put her through." When the phone on his desk rang, he took a deep breath and slowly picked up the receiver.

"Hello, Thomas, this is Diane." She didn't need to say her name; he would have recognized her voice anywhere.

"Yes, Diane. How are you?" He tried to sound distantly polite, nothing more.

"I've been quite well." The hesitation in her voice was almost undetectable. "I wondered when you might be planning your next trip to the States."

He stopped breathing and felt certain his heart missed a good three beats. She had sent him away, and he had accepted that as her final word. Was she now, after all this time, reconsidering his proposition?

He cleared his throat and began cautiously. "There was—is, actually—a possibility of a trip sometime within the next month. The timing isn't crucial."

"I see," she said.

"Is something wrong?"

"Not wrong, really. I just would like to talk with you about something that affects both of us. I'd rather not do it over the telephone."

Now he knew! She was about to welcome him back

into her life, *on his own terms!* But she wanted to
negotiate details, possibly find ways to protect herself.
That was fine by him.

"I'll arrange the business end of the trip around
you. Will next Saturday be soon enough?"

"Yes," she said, "just call to let me know what
time you'll arrive."

He loved the soft timbre of her voice; it was so
soothing, so accepting of life. But she hung up before
he could tell her how happy he was they'd be together
again.

It was a typical fall day in New England—gray,
raining, a snapping cold wind off the ocean—when
Thomas pulled the sedan up in front of her house. He
went to the kitchen door and knocked. She opened it
almost immediately.

Diane was wearing an oxford-style shirt over her
jeans, her dark hair pulled back with a stretchy thing
Allison called a scrunchie. She looked fresh as the
new day, her cheeks aglow as if she'd just scrubbed
them. Her eyes were bright, but seemed a little sad
when she greeted him. He was glad it would be only
a matter of minutes before he'd be able to set them
sparkling again.

"I've made coffee," she said, swerving away from
him when he stepped toward her, expecting to take
her in his arms. "It's decaf."

"That sounds good." He took a seat at the kitchen
table, resigned to waiting until she was ready to be
held. She'd set two places. He liked the cozy feeling
of the room, sunshine-yellow with sunflowers on the
oven mitts, the dish towel and refrigerator magnets.

He could feel comfortable in a little room like this, with her…and he would as often as he could.

He had to stop himself from grinning in anticipation of the next few hours they'd spend together, working out their relationship, making up for lost time in her bedroom. The children were nowhere in sight; she must have sent them off somewhere with Elly. He felt himself respond to his imagination's suggestions of how she would look when she took off that neatly pressed blouse for him.

Diane set a steaming mug of coffee in front of him and slid a plate of fresh muffins within his reach. "I'm glad you've had a change of heart," he said softly. "I've missed you."

She sat down and frowned at him. "I've missed you, too, Thomas. But before you say anything else, I need to tell you something."

He smiled good-naturedly. "Fire away." Nothing could dampen his mood. Nothing. He had her back.

"I'm going to have your baby, Thomas."

He could have sworn he'd misheard her. There was a strange echo effect in the kitchen. Or perhaps he was so overjoyed at seeing her again, his imagination was playing tricks on him.

"Did you hear me?" she asked.

"I…well, I'm not sure that you said what I thought you said." His smile teetered a bit.

"I said, I'm pregnant with your child."

The coffee mug floated halfway between his lips and the tabletop. "That's impossible."

"I would have thought so, too."

She explained her theory of the possible moment of conception. He listened numbly and could think of no argument. His mind simply went blank.

"You've verified this with a physician?"

She nodded, cupping her hands around her own mug and gazing down into the rising steam. "I'm a little more than three months along. The baby should be born in March. The twentieth, if I'm on time."

"Dear Lord."

Diane looked up at him, her eyes snapping with sudden anger. "That's all you have to say?"

"I'm just— It's a complete surprise. I'm sorry, I—"

She waved off his stammered apologies, and her eyes softened. "I guess I didn't exactly break the news gently. Listen, it's not a catastrophe. I'm fine with being pregnant. More than fine. I love children, and four will be no more work than three. The older ones can help out, too," she added, her energy seeming to grow as she spoke. "Of course, it will take some time for my parents and Jacob to deal with this, particularly when I tell them who the father is. Allison will support me no matter what, but—"

A sharp stab of terror ripped through him. "You intend to tell Jacob?"

"Of course. Do you think I'm going to keep something like this a secret from my family?"

He put down the mug and dropped his head into his hands, slick with sweat he hadn't felt until then. "No, of course not. Forgive me I don't know what I was thinking. But Jacob..." He sighed. She was carrying a child because of his carelessness. He was responsible, and he would face up to his duty. "I will, of course, do what's right by you and the child. We can marry as soon as you—"

"No!" she cut him off. "This isn't about forcing you into marriage."

"But you...the baby should—"

She gripped the edge of the table and looked him square in the eyes. "I don't need a long-distance husband...or boyfriend. But I do need help with medical bills. That only seems fair, don't you think?"

He nodded fervently. "Absolutely, but—"

"But nothing," she said crisply. "Here is what we'll do...."

Thomas walked out of the little house on the Connecticut shore in a daze. He'd learned to accept life's twists and turns, its disappointments, even its sometimes cruel sense of humor. But to be told he would become a father—the one eventuality he had avoided all of his adult life—that was just too bloody much of a shock to his system!

Still, all he felt was concern and the deepest admiration for Diane. He didn't hate her for so casually announcing that she was ready to tell the world he'd fathered the child she was carrying. He didn't think her request for help with the baby's expenses was outrageous at all. In fact, he had told her that even though she refused his hasty marriage proposal, he would support her and all of her children for as long as she wished.

She had quietly, proudly, turned him down.

Her strength and resolve to keep his baby and raise it with as much love as she lavished on her other three moved him more deeply than he could ever have foreseen. It was as if part of him was being welcomed and cherished, mothered and loved. And he found he liked that feeling, though it was coming late in his life.

Thomas spent the trip back to Elbia in deep

thought. He slept some of the time on the plane. Mostly he stared out the tiny square window beside his leather seat and saw Diane's face. He envisioned her lovely body, slowly swelling to accommodate his child. She grew more beautiful in his mind's eye with each passing day. And he knew his baby would be strong and healthy, nourished by her body…just as he had been nourished by her love.

Love, he thought. The word had always mystified and eluded him. Now he felt so close to understanding it, he could almost wrap his fingers around it and draw it toward him.

He remembered the glimmer in Diane's tear-misted eyes as she'd bade him goodbye at her door. She'd allowed him one chaste kiss on her soft lips as she'd looked up at him. And now he knew what that look meant. She loved him, although pride hadn't allowed her to say the words.

She loved him. And she was carrying his child.

But what did he feel for her, other than the respect due the mother of his child? Did he still desire her? Absolutely. Was there yet another emotion lurking behind others, beckoning to him? Did he love her, too?

He thrust that troubling thought from his mind. Whether or not love had anything to do with his present situation, his first duty remained to protect and serve the royal family. He couldn't simply walk away from that responsibility. And nothing of his past had changed. He was still his mother's son. How could he promise he'd always be around for Diane and their baby when he knew in his heart that he was fated to leave them one day?

It was dawn when the jet landed at the airport in

Vienna. The helicopter took him to the castle grounds, and he strode from the landing pad, through the garden where Allison was playing with the little prince and princess. He gave each child an avuncular pat on the head and Allison a nervous smile to cover his guilt, then plowed on up the petal-strewn path to the castle. Jacob was in his office, already at work.

"Ah, you're back," he said, folding the newspaper he'd been reading.

"Yes." Thomas had asked Diane to let him be the one to tell Jacob about her condition. He had rehearsed a variety of approaches to the subject, but he couldn't remember any of them now. He opted for an incoherent stream of babble. "Sir, I've seen Diane again. No, I didn't sleep with her, but what I have to say is…well, it's connected in a way with—" He groaned. "This isn't going to be easy for either of us, sir, but there's no way of avoiding the truth." Jacob pressed his hands over the newsprint and looked up with a puzzled frown, while Thomas plunged on. "She's carrying a child. Mine. The baby is mine."

There, he'd said it. He'd never get a Nobel Peace Prize for his speech, but at least he'd gotten it out.

"You're mad," Jacob stated.

"I wish I were, Your Highness. I never wanted to hurt Diane or cause her distress of any kind. But there it is. She is three months pregnant and I am the father. She will keep the baby, and I'll help her with expenses. I promise that she and the child will have everything they need."

The muscles in Jacob's face twitched with fury, but he said nothing for a moment. Then he opened his mouth and Thomas anticipated his next words.

"I asked her to marry me. She refused."

"Of course she refused you!" Jacob bellowed.

Thomas's mouth dropped wide. "Of course?" he echoed weakly. Was he that poor a catch?

"If your proposal sounded anything like the apologetic drivel you've just handed me, what else would a woman do?"

Thomas stared at him, confused. "I'm sorry, sir. I don't understand."

Jacob pressed thumb and forefinger over the bridge of his nose and shot up from his desk to pace the floor, his heels coming down hard on the Persian silk carpet that stretched from one side of the room to the other. "Did you tell her you loved her and wanted to spend your life with her?"

"Well, no, I—"

"Why not? You care about the woman, don't you? Why can't you tell her how you feel, Thomas?"

He did care about Diane, that was true. He supposed, now that he thought about it, he always had—from the moment they met. He'd never felt happier or liked himself as much as when he was around her. He was fond of her children, and he felt deep within his soul that he would cherish the child they'd made. But did he *love* her?

"My first loyalty has always been to you and the royal family, sir," he blurted out.

"Well, maybe it's about time some changes were made around here!" Jacob barked.

Thomas rocked back on his heels as if he'd been punched in the stomach. "Sir?"

"It may not have been something you've noticed, but the playboy bachelor you used to rescue from brawls in pubs has grown up and has a family of his own now."

"Well, of course." Thomas laughed stiffly. "But now I must protect not only you, but the queen and the wee ones."

"That's not what I meant. I can well afford to hire a dozen bodyguards and social secretaries."

"You're saying you don't need me anymore?"

"I'm saying I still want you as a friend, a brother in spirit," Jacob explained, stopping his pacing and turning to face Thomas across the claret field of silk beneath their feet. "I don't need you to be on call twenty-four hours a day. Allison and I have talked about this. She's right. You deserve a life of your own."

It was a radical idea to Thomas—a life apart from his royals. A family of his own? No, that was too much to hope for. "That doesn't change who I am," he said grimly.

"Who do you *think* you are?" Jacob asked, watching his expression intently.

"I...I am a man who has never stayed with one woman longer than three months."

"You believe you'll desert Diane and your child as your mother deserted you and your brothers?" Jacob guessed.

Thomas stared at the young king, unable to turn away from the steady, blue eyes. "Yes. I think it's possible."

"Anything is possible. Are you willing to stake your and Diane's happiness against a fear?"

Thomas had never thought of it in that way.

"I think of you as a very different man," Jacob said in a quieter voice as he stepped toward him. "You are a man who has been loyal to me for over a dozen years, Thomas Smythe. You have stood by me and my family through the most trying times. I can't imagine a man like that doing less for his own family.''

Thomas swallowed and blinked at the newness of the idea Jacob had laid before him. It was as if he'd offered his trusted servant and friend the gift of a beautiful piece of land and said, Now build your house on this and it will be strong.

Thomas drew a deep breath, then let it out and immediately turned toward the door.

''Where are you going?'' Jacob asked.

Thomas grinned to himself. ''To court the woman who will be my wife.''

Ten

Diane finished her inventory of aisle four and clicked the cap back on her pen. It had been a long day, and she was glad it was nearly over. She couldn't wait to go home and relieve Elly, spend some time with her kids and soak in a steaming tub of sudsy water. Tuesday nights they all took turns choosing board games. Even little Gare joined in.

Tucking her clipboard under one arm, she turned toward the rear of the store and took one step into a wall of flowers.

At least it seemed an entire wall.

Until she stepped back to get a better look and found it was only an enormous bouquet of mums, roses, daisies and baby's breath, held out by a huge hand. She leaned to one side to look around the blooms at the owner of the hand.

"Thomas? What are you doing here?"

He lowered the bouquet just enough to speak over it. "I understand that a mother's state of mind affects an unborn child."

"Huh?"

"If you're happy, the baby will be content."

"Oh," she said studying his serious expression. "Well, yes, I suppose I've read that somewhere, too."

"So it's important for the baby that you're relaxed and not worrying about anything."

She started walking toward the office to turn in her stock count. "I guess."

"And I know you like flowers."

"True."

"So, do they make you happy?"

She stopped and spun around to face him. "What's this really about?"

He shrugged innocently. "Nothing. I just want to make sure you're in good spirits…for the baby's sake."

Sliding her clipboard beneath the plexiglass partition at customer service, Diane nodded at her boss to indicate she was finished and leaving for the day. She punched out and took off her bright-red smock and draped it over her arm. All she'd brought with her were her keys, and those were in the smock's pocket. Thomas was still holding the flowers out for her to take.

"Oh, what the heck." She sighed and thrust her face into the blooms and breathed in the delicious perfume. "Thank you…on behalf of the baby. They are beautiful." They were out the door and nearly at her car when something odd occurred to her. "I thought you were flying straight back to Elbia the night before last.''

"I was—I mean, I did.''

"And you're back again already?''

"I have very pressing business on this side of the Atlantic.''

"I see.'' She shook her head as she opened the car door and slid into the driver's seat. It was early in her pregnancy, but she was already beginning to feel a little unwieldy. With her other babies, she hadn't even started to show until her fifth month. "Well, thanks for the posies. I'd better get home. The kids are probably bouncing off the walls by now.''

Thomas put his hand out to stop the car door from closing between them. She looked up, and his eyes seemed darkly mysterious.

"What?''

"I've been invited to join the family for a game of Clue.''

"You what?'' she demanded.

"The children. I stopped by the house looking for you,'' Thomas explained. "They told me you'd be here and asked if I could come back and play with them when you got home.''

"They did, did they?'' She squinted at him. There was definitely something fishy going on.

"Aren't you on an important mission?''

"Very important,'' he said solemnly.

"Don't you think you should get to it then?''

"In good time,'' he said quietly. "In good time.''

"Well, I have to stop for pizza on the way home. I'll meet you back at the house.''

He grinned at her and carefully shut her car door.

"I'll pick up dinner. You go home and put your feet up until I get there. Do the children like the works?"

"Buy a large, plain cheese for them and a medium veggie special for me...for us," she said, correcting herself. "Angie's is the best. It's just around the corner from my house."

The scent of the flowers on the seat beside her seemed to seep into her sore muscles and relax them. She had never seen such lush blooms in her life; the colors were so vibrant, they reminded her of a flower cart she'd seen in Elbia. Thomas couldn't have brought the bouquet all the way from Europe, could he? Of course not. They must have been a spur-of-the-moment purchase, the result of an attack of male guilt.

But they were unbelievably lovely....

Diane dismissed Elly, who asked if Thomas had found her okay at the store. "He's such a hunk," she commented, rolling her eyes as she stepped out the door into the chill air. "Don't you think so, Mrs. Fields?"

"Good night, Elly." Laughing, she pushed the girl out the door. "We'll see you tomorrow."

The children were already in their pj's, and they'd taken the game from the closet and set it up in the middle of the living room floor. Diane spread newspapers over the coffee table. They would sit on the floor around it and eat between turns at the game. It would be a fun evening. She wouldn't mind waiting a couple of hours for her bath.

Thomas arrived soon after. She'd only had time to change out of her work clothes into a pair of lounging pajamas Allison had insisted on buying her. She'd never had silk pajamas, because they seemed impractical and chilly for New England. But these felt remarkably soft and cozy next to her skin.

She cut and served the pizza on paper plates, and Thomas poured plastic cups of soda for all. They played for an hour and a half, and Diane felt as if she'd never enjoyed an evening so much. She worried that Thomas might try to linger after the children were asleep, but while she put the children to bed, he cleaned up the living room and tossed the empty plates and pizza boxes into the trash. When she came out, all the work had been done, and he was standing near the kitchen door.

"I'd better leave now," he said. "You need your rest."

"And so do you if you have meetings tomorrow."

Nodding, he picked up her fingertips, brought them to his lips, kissed them lightly, then was out the door before she realized what had happened. She watched him walk away, his wide shoulders filling a space in the darkness, his stride strong and determined. Elly was right. He was a hunk all right. It was just too bad that he didn't love her.

The next day she was getting ready for work when someone knocked at her kitchen door. Elly's early, she thought with relief. Elly, being a typical teenager, would sleep until noon unless someone dragged her out of bed.

But it wasn't Elly.

Diane stared at Thomas as he walked in and plopped a bag of groceries on the table.

"What is this?"

"I'm filling in for Elly today," he announced as he started hauling items out of the bags and placing them in her refrigerator. "She called to say she wasn't feeling well."

"She called *you* instead of *me* to cancel?"

"She didn't want to wake the children," he explained, then held up a shrink-wrapped package. "Blueberry crumpets! Imagine that, in an American store."

"Imagine," she repeated skeptically.

Something was definitely wrong with this picture. But she didn't have time to argue, so she let Thomas have his way and stay with the children while she went off to put in six hours at the store.

Over the following days, Diane's suspicions grew. Thomas never seemed to be out of her sight for more than a few hours at a time. He stayed at the house as late as she let him stay, which crept closer and closer to midnight. He returned as soon as possible the next day.

Each time they met, she questioned him about his mission. He only smiled and assured her he was taking care of what needed to be done.

Diane felt comfortable around Thomas, but torn as well. The more often he was around, the more she felt aware of how empty the little house would seem when he left. The children loved him, and he was so very good with them. She was saddened, just thinking how hard it would be for them when he was gone. She intentionally didn't ask when he thought he would be finished in the States and would return to Elbia. And he said nothing about it, either.

Each day when she came home from the store, she looked at the flowers he'd brought to the store that first day. They stood in a vase on her kitchen table, but never seemed to wilt or turn brown. After a while she realized that he was replacing faded blossoms with new ones. And for every day he was in Nanticoke, another rose appeared, until as two weeks approached, only roses remained, and all the other blooms had disappeared.

She said nothing and wondered what Thomas was trying to say to her. But she was too afraid to ask.

One evening he appeared as he usually did, within minutes of her returning home. Elly had come to expect him, too, but this day the baby-sitter didn't gather up her Walkman, audio tapes, teen magazines and fingernail polish in preparation for a hasty departure.

Thomas set a pizza box on the kitchen table and winked at the teenager. "Pepperoni, onions and green peppers, just as you ordered, m'lady."

Diane scowled at the two of them, sensing something was up. "I take it you two have been in communication before I came home?"

Elly giggled. "I'm staying to watch the tribe a few hours extra tonight. Thomas's treat."

"Oh?" Diane raised a questioning brow at him.

"I thought you might like a quiet dinner on the water, seeing it's been a long week, and I'll be—"

"Don't say it," she said quickly, a lump swelling in her throat. "You'll be leaving soon."

"Yes. I will." He fixed her with a look she couldn't read.

She told herself she'd known this day would come. But that didn't make it any easier. "Give me a few minutes to change," she murmured, and hastily dashed for her bedroom to hide the tears welling in her eyes.

They arrived at Sonny's, a deceptively casual-sounding restaurant located only five miles along the shore. A deck lit by strings of tiny white bulbs looked over the water. Although it was a Friday night, and the restaurant was a very popular place, they were the only couple seated outside.

"It's beautiful out here, and so crowded inside. I wonder why no one wants a table outside," she commented after the host seated them and lit the candle on their table before quickly hurrying away.

Thomas shrugged. "All the more moonlight for us."

She squinted at him across the table. First flowers, then multiplying roses, now an al fresco dinner in a trendy restaurant?

"You paid them to give us the deck to ourselves," she accused.

He blinked complacently at her across the linen-covered table and reached out a hand to cover hers. "Does that upset you?"

"No," she answered truthfully, "it is sort of nice to have you to myself...since you're leaving so soon. And then there's—" she shrugged "—never mind."

He enclosed her trembling fingers in his. "Tell me what you're thinking," he whispered.

She was tearing up again. "I can't."

"Why not?"

"Damn it, Thomas, don't you know?" She loved him, and he was leaving her. Again. And she knew she'd never care about another man the way she cared for him. Not ever.

"Would it help if I went first?"

She looked at him, taken by surprise. "I thought you'd already made your feelings about me...about us, very clear."

"As clear as I could at the time...but not clear enough. Not for you or for myself."

"I see." But she didn't, not really. "Go on," she murmured.

He looked out across the waves gently lapping at the pillars of a nearby wharf, streaked in shafts of moonlight. His face tightened with effort for a moment, then smoothed as he found the words he needed. His thumb absently stroked the curve of her palm.

"I believed I knew myself so well I could predetermine my whole life. I would someday be the Earl of Sussex, exchanging my minor title for a more-important one when my father died. I would continue investing my inheritance to ensure I would be able to lead a life of leisure when I chose to do so. I would remain in Jacob's employ as long as he tolerated me." He smiled at this, and she was sure it was because he knew Jacob's loyalty to him equaled his own to Jacob. "And I would never marry," he finished solemnly.

Her heart fluttered, though she couldn't have said why. "Are you saying some part of your master plan was wrong?"

"Very definitely it was wrong."

"Are you leaving the king?" she asked.

"No," he said. "I'm getting married."

The sorrow in her heart was paralyzing. So that was why he'd come. To settle his paternal obligations so that he could, in good conscience, take another woman as his wife. She shattered inside. She might have been a delicate crystal vase, crushed in his huge hand. She pulled her fingertips out from beneath his and clutched her hands in her lap and couldn't stop the tears now, no matter how hard she tried.

"Diane, don't."

She squeezed her eyes shut and shook her head violently. She couldn't speak, couldn't make herself get up out of the chair and walk back through the crowded dining room, which was the only way out of the restaurant. But she couldn't stay here, much less eat a meal.

Why couldn't she be as casual and civilized about their parting as he was being? Why did it matter so much—being with one man? She despised herself for being weak, yet the tears kept coming.

Diane became aware that he was kneeling beside her, and a second later his arms came around her and he was hugging her to his chest and whispering something to her she couldn't hear above her own anguished sobs.

She couldn't bear to listen to his parting words. She would explode if she didn't escape within seconds! Yet somehow his voice sank through the layers of desperate grief.

"Open your eyes...open your eyes...open your eyes," he was repeating in his wonderfully gruff baritone. "Diane, trust me...this once."

She shook her head miserably but let her eyelids drift up, and he dropped something into her lap. Through a blur of tears she saw the black velvet box. It took nearly a full minute before its meaning registered. Even then, she didn't dare believe.

Was he toying with her? Offering once more to give her something he knew he had no right to promise? Or maybe this was just a parting gift, something to soften the blow....

She squeezed her eyes shut once more, then opened them all the way. "A man engaged to one woman shouldn't be giving another woman expensive presents."

"I'm not," he said firmly.

"I won't open that," she told him.

"Why?"

"If it's a ring, it will break my heart." As if it wasn't already lying in shards at her feet.

"I don't understand."

"Because you can't stand behind it. It doesn't mean what it should."

"Ask me what it means," he said, his tone a challenge.

Diane shook her head. She wasn't that brave.

"Ask me," he said in a low, insistent growl and kissed the near corner of her lips still wet with her tears.

She drew a deep breath and let it out with a sense that fate had taken over the scene. How could she fight him when she felt so helpless? "All right. What does whatever's in that jeweler's box mean to you?"

He slid his arms down around her so that he could manipulate the hinged cover. A flash of diamonds and rubies took her breath away. If this was a parting gift, it had at least cost him a sizable chunk of his estate. She couldn't speak. She couldn't even breathe.

"I love you, Diane. There was no woman on this earth I've ever wanted to spend my life with…before you. There will never be another. If you say no, I will spend the rest of my days a lonely, bitter man."

It took her several minutes of replaying his words through her mind to absorb them. Then tears started afresh.

"How…why…how can you say this now? It wasn't true a month ago."

"It was true, I just didn't understand. I needed to sort some things out for myself. It took losing you to make me see what had been standing in front of me all of this time. I loved you from the moment Allison introduced us. You were married, with three young children—forbidden territory. I still wanted you. But I couldn't have you."

"But later…when you knew I was divorced…"

"Sometimes it takes a man a long time to rearrange the rules he's lived his whole life by." He drew her close and kissed her on the mouth, then pressed her cheek to his shoulder, and she could smell the spicy scent of him above the salt of the ocean. "I'm sorry it took me so long to come around. But please don't turn me down because I was a fool then. I know who I am and what I want now. We need to be together. Forever."

She was stunned and shaking too hard to trust her feelings. He pushed her gently back to look into her eyes. "I love you, Diane. Does it come too late? Have you stopped loving me?"

"I never said I did," she said.

The light in his dark eyes faded. "I see."

"But I do," she said quickly. "I do love you, Thomas…with all my heart. I just wish I hadn't been so transparent."

He grinned, looking relieved. "You've never been that, only honest. Another reason why I love you." His hands were moving now with purpose, holding the little box with one hand, slipping the ring out with the other. She watched as he slid it down over the fourth finger of her left hand. A diamond solitaire picked up color from the encircling rubies, sparkling with pale pink highlights. She'd never owned even one small diamond. She felt as if she had an entire jewelry store on her finger.

"Can you afford this?" she asked breathlessly.

He grinned and nodded. "If you don't like it. We'll get something else. With your dark hair...I thought the rubies..." Emotion choked off the rest. "You haven't said yes yet." His dark eyes waited, pleaded, hoped.

"Yes," she whispered. "Yes, I'll marry you, Thomas Smythe." And she threw her arms around his big neck and wept for joy and disbelief that her wildest fantasies had been exceeded ten times over.

Their wedding was, strangely enough, grander than Allison's had been to Jacob, for that had been carried out in secret in a Manhattan lawyer's office to avoid the press. Jacob insisted that Diane and Thomas gather up her children and fly to Europe to be married in the chapel at the castle. Her parents joined them there, along with close to 100 other guests, although Diane would have been happy with just a simple family wedding back in Nanticoke. Still, she was gratified to see that Thomas welcomed an audience for their nuptials. It was as if he wanted to prove to her that he no longer feared the vows he'd so long dodged. His "I do" boomed through the nave of the ancient church. When he took her in his arms, at the moment the priest announced them as husband and wife, he kissed her so long and hard she hardly had enough breath left to make it down the aisle and into the garden.

It seemed amazingly easy to believe that they

would be together from that day forward. Diane accepted a position with the royal charities, which would be challenging but allow her ample time to have her baby and be with her older children. Thomas offered to live anywhere she liked, buying them a house roomy enough for a family of six. But Diane was of a practical mind.

"To do our jobs, we need to live in Elbia, at least for most of the year. You'll still be with Jacob, right?"

"I would like to continue on his staff, although we've already spoken of ways to cut my hours to give me time for my family." He said the words *my family* with glowing pride that echoed that of fathers throughout time. He had accepted her own children with such open joy she had no doubt he would always do what was best for them.

It was decided the Smythes would have a private apartment in the west wing of the castle, including Thomas's old chambers and several additional rooms for the children. A small kitchen and extra bathrooms would be added for their convenience.

As for Gary, her ex, he wrote to Diane one more time, asking for start-up money for his business. Thomas responded with a check in exchange for Gary's promise in writing, that he would stay out of their lives forever.

A few months later Thomas found Diane sitting in the garden, a rose lying across her lap. It was the color of those he'd added to her bouquet when he'd courted her, and he knew she was thinking of those days.

"Any regrets?" he asked.

She looked up at him as if she'd known he was

there, but was surprised by his question. "No. Why do you ask?"

"You seem happy. I just wanted to be sure."

"I'm in heaven," she murmured, pulling him down to kiss him energetically on the lips.

He sat down beside her on the stone bench and picked up the rose, not even feeling the thorns through the thick pads of his fingers. His glance took in the fullness of her belly, and he felt warm and protective.

"You're feeling well, aren't you?"

She smiled up at him. "Perfect."

"You aren't homesick for Connecticut?"

She shook her head. "I'll look forward to a few weeks' vacation there, once in a while. But no, I don't miss it. It seems more important that we're together...wherever that may be."

He nodded. Yes, that was how he felt, too. He could make a home anywhere with this woman. Geography had little to do with love, when it finally came.

"There is one thing I'd like," Diane said tentatively, bringing his attention back to her.

He tightened at the subtle longing in her voice. What had he forgotten to do for her?

"Tell me," he said, already determined to please.

"Stop treating me as if I'll break when we make love."

He laughed. "But the baby...!"

She smiled sweetly at him. "You won't hurt me...or the baby."

"You're certain?"

She pulled his arm around her and pressed herself against him. Her full breasts warmed his chest; her beautifully expressive mouth settled urgently over his. She slipped her hands beneath his shirt and caressed him. His body responded with a rapid burst of heat.

"Even when I'm bigger than the royal stables," she said, her eyes twinkling mischievously, "I think we can come up with ways to please each other."

He chuckled low in his throat. "Oh, you do, do you?"

"Perhaps we should experiment now?" she suggested. "Just to be sure."

"Perhaps we should, Lady Smythe."

He brought her to her feet and kissed her a dozen times before they reached their chamber. And as they made love that winter afternoon, he knew that no one and nothing would ever take this joy, this woman from his arms.

*   *   *   *   *

▼ SILHOUETTE
DESIRE ®

AVAILABLE FROM 21ST SEPTEMBER 2001

HER PERFECT MAN Mary Lynn Baxter

Conservative Bryce Burnette wasn't ready for a wife but one look at Katherine Mays and his life went careering off its steady course. If only he could control their burning desire…

IRRESISTIBLE YOU Barbara Boswell

Luke Minteer expected to hate jury duty, but he was rather enjoying himself. It couldn't have anything to do with the sexy, single, nine months pregnant woman who sat beside him…could it?

ROUGH AROUND THE EDGES Marie Ferrarella

Shawn O'Rourke had to marry to stay in the country and who better to ask than new single mum, Kitt Dawson? He couldn't promise forever, but even he wouldn't deny the searing passion between them…

MAROONED WITH A MARINE Maureen Child

Stranded in the middle of a hurricane with the one man she never wanted to see again, Karen Beckett needed all her strength to resist Gunnery Sergeant Sam Paretti. Because to surrender to their urgent need would mean exposing her past…

ONE SNOWBOUND WEEKEND… Christy Lockhart

Dazed and injured, Angie Burton battled a blizzard to get home. But Angie wasn't prepared for the icy reception that awaited her—or the realisation that she had no memory of walking out on the man she loved.

HIS SHELTERING ARMS Kristi Gold

His job was to keep Erin Brailey safe. But first, security expert Zach Miller had to convince the sultry beauty that she needed his protection…while keeping his desire for her hidden!

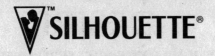

MONTANA
WEDDINGS
A legacy of passion...
Two generations of brides
Three marriages of convenience...
Buy Montana Weddings and
save £1.00 off Montana
Brides – Lone Stallion's Lady
Christine Rimmer
Jennifer Greene
Cheryl St.John

Silhouette Stars

Born this month

Gloria Estefan, Charlie Sheen, Raquel Welch,
Buddy Holly, Peter Sellers, Maria Callas,
Oliver Stone, John Dankworth, Ray Charles,
Olivia Newton-John.

Star of the month

Virgo

A positive year in which many of your dreams
can come true, especially in the area of personal
relationships where greater commitment will
lead to true happiness. Finances may need a
cautious approach in the first part of the year if
you are to reap the rewards on offer later.

SILH/HR/0901a

Libra

Career matters are highlighted and your efforts will not go unnoticed. Romance is also on your mind and you could attract some welcome attention.

Scorpio

A complete change of scene would suit you right now, however practically that may be difficult to organise. Try taking up a new sport or hobby to change your surroundings and supply the lift you need.

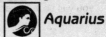 **Sagittarius**

An upbeat month with plenty of social events to keep you busy. A new acquaintance brings an air of mystery that you may find intriguing, however all may not be what it seems.

Capricorn

The pace of life should quieten down and there will be opportunities to relax and enjoy the results of recent achievements. Finances are looking good and you should be able to afford something you have wanted for a long time.

 **Aquarius**

A more cautious approach to life may be needed this month; taking everything at face value could lead to disappointment. Late in the month good news could give good reason to celebrate.

Pisces

Life is definitely on the way up; you should start feeling more settled and in control. A social event could lead to someone new entering your life. This person may well become a lasting friend.

Aries

Recent changes in your life, although confusing, should have left you feeling more positive and able to move on. Romantic encounters early in the month set your pulse racing. Could this be the real thing?

Taurus

You need to stop having good ideas and concentrate on the ones you have already had. By continuing along the same path you will ultimately make brilliant progress this month. Lady Luck is on your side and this could mean some financial gain.

 Gemini

A social and happy month in which there is little to dull your shine. You are in demand, so relax and enjoy this well earned spell of success.

Cancer

Potentially a month of important developments, however you need to be receptive to all that is on offer. Listen carefully to those close and take on board their point of view as in harmony you will be stronger.

 Leo

Don't be fooled by the quiet start to the month as life is about to take off, you should be full of energy and able to rise to the challenge. Romantically the month ends on a high note as you realise just how important you really are.

**Look out for more
Silhouette Stars next month**

FREE
2 BOOKS
AND A SURPRISE GIFT!

We would like to take this opportunity to thank you for reading this Silhouette® book by offering you the chance to take TWO more specially selected titles from the Desire™ series absolutely FREE! We're also making this offer to introduce you to the benefits of the Reader Service™—

- ★ FREE home delivery
- ★ FREE monthly Newsletter
- ★ FREE gifts and competitions
- ★ Exclusive Reader Service discounts
- ★ Books available before they're in the shops

Accepting these FREE books and gift places you under no obligation to buy; you may cancel at any time, even after receiving your free shipment. Simply complete your details below and return the entire page to the address below. **You don't even need a stamp!**

YES! Please send me 2 free Desire books and a surprise gift. I understand that unless you hear from me, I will receive 4 superb new titles every month for just £2.80 each, postage and packing free. I am under no obligation to purchase any books and may cancel my subscription at any time. The free books and gift will be mine to keep in any case.

D1ZEC

Ms/Mrs/Miss/Mr ....Initials................................

BLOCK CAPITALS PLEASE

Surname...

Address...

....

....Postcode ....

Send this whole page to:
UK: FREEPOST CN81, Croydon, CR9 3WZ
EIRE: PO Box 4546, Kilcock, County Kildare (stamp required)